It was Canyon O'Grady's first day in the Wyoming town. It looked like it might be his last.

His first mistake was getting in an argument with Red Atkins. His second was following Red's lead in dropping his six-gun to the saloon floor.

That lost him his one advantage over this bully boy who looked like he was made of solid steel.

The pretty bar girl gave Canyon a farewell smile. The bartender asked Canyon to pay for his beer before the action started.

Red Atkins made the message even plainer. "Come on, friend," he said, beckoning O'Grady forward with sausagelike fingers. "Come and get your back broken."

Little Bend was laying out the welcome mat for Canyon O'Grady—and was about to lay his corpse right on top of it. . . .

CANYON O'GRADY RIDES ON

WYOMING CONSPIRACY

by
Jon Sharpe

A SIGNET BOOK

SIGNET
Published by the Penguin Group
Penguin Books USA Inc., 375 Hudson Street,
New York, New York 10014, U.S.A.
Penguin Books Ltd, 27 Wrights Lane,
London W8 5TZ, England
Penguin Books Australia Ltd, Ringwood,
Victoria, Australia
Penguin Books Canada Ltd, 10 Alcorn Avenue,
Toronto, Ontario, Canada M4V 3B2
Penguin Books (N.Z.) Ltd, 182–190 Wairau Road,
Auckland 10, New Zealand

Penguin Books Ltd, Registered Offices:
Harmondsworth, Middlesex, England

First published by Signet,
an imprint of New American Library,
a division of Penguin Books USA Inc.

First Printing, September, 1992
10 9 8 7 6 5 4 3 2 1

Canyon O'Grady

His was a heritage of blackguards and poets, fighters and lovers, men who could draw a pistol and bed a lass with the same ease.

Freedom was a cry seared into Canyon O'Grady, justice a banner of his heart.

With the great wave of those who fled to America, the new land of hope and heartbreak, solace and savagery, he came to ride the untamed wildness of the Old West.

With a smile or a six-gun, Canyon O'Grady became a name feared by some and welcomed by others, but remembered by all . . .

Little Bend, Wyoming . . . a quiet town in frontier cattle country. But unbridled greed and deadly conspiracy bred behind closed doors in this peaceful home-on-the-range . . .

1

When Canyon O'Grady rode into the town of Little Bend, Wyoming, it struck him how inappropriate the name was for the town. Little Bend was far from "little." It was a good-sized town that gave every outward indication that it was still growing. Some of the buildings had obviously been standing for some time, and were showing signs of age, but many of the buildings in town had obviously been erected recently. Indeed, there were several buildings that were still being built. O'Grady could hear the sounds of hammering and sawing as he rode down the main street, looking for the livery stable.

Many western towns were made up of two streets that crossed in the center, and not much else. Little Bend was different. There were so many streets intersecting with the main street that O'Grady finally had to stop and ask where the livery stable was.

"You're on Front Street," a helpful lad of about thirteen told him. "Go back to Wyoming Street and make a left. The livery stable is at the very end."

"Thanks, son."

"You plannin' on livin' here, Mister?"

"No, son," O'Grady said. "I'm just passing through. Thanks for the directions."

"I got a real pretty sister, Mister," the boy said. "She's only eighteen, and she's still a virgin. If you're interested—"

"That's okay," O'Grady said, cutting the boy off. "I'll look for my own women."

O'Grady turned his horse and rode back to Wyoming Street, shaking his head. In town five minutes and already he'd been offered somebody's "virgin" sister. Some things never changed. Even a growing town like Little Bend still had its share of street hustlers.

O'Grady successfully located the livery stable and made the arrangements to have his horse cared for over the next few days.

"Gonna stay awhile, huh?" the liveryman asked, accepting Cormac's reins while O'Grady removed his saddlebags and rifle from his saddle.

"Maybe a few days," O'Grady said. He hoped he'd only be staying a few days—or even less.

"It's a nice town," the man went on. "People here would give ya the shirt off their backs."

"Or their sister," O'Grady said.

"What's that?"

"Nothing," O'Grady said. "Can you direct me to the nearest hotel?"

"The best hotel in town—"

"Not the best," O'Grady said, "just the closest."

"Well, that'd be the Overland House," the man said. "Go back the way you came, then keep going when you get to Front Street. It'll be on the left."

"Okay, thanks."

O'Grady tossed his saddlebags over one shoulder, lifted his rifle and left the livery.

Twenty miles outside of town, Brenda Edderly was standing in front of the huge main house that was the cornerstone of the Edderly Ranch. It was easily the biggest ranch in the territory, and she had been running it since the death of her father two months earlier. Standing with her was the foreman, Pete Gentry. Gentry had worked for Harlan Edderly for ten years, the last three as the ranch's foreman.

Brenda was twenty-three, tall and full-bodied, with a cascade of tawny hair that fell almost to her waist. In every way she was a beautiful, mature woman, but many people—Pete Gentry included—felt she was too young to run a spread the size of the Edderly Ranch.

Gentry himself had just about grown up on the Edderly Ranch. He was hired on when he was eighteen as a ranch hand, and had worked his way up to foreman at the fairly young age of twenty-nine. He was a tall, broad-shouldered man with almost no hips. He was considered by the women in town to be one of Little Bend's most eligible bachelors.

"Brenda," he said, "if you'd just leave everything to me—"

"Pete, I appreciate the offer, but this ranch has always been run by an Edderly, and it will continue to be run by an Edderly."

"No offense, Brenda, but you are kind of young—"

"I've been hearing that for two months, Pete," Brenda said, "and I'm tired of it. When Dad gave you the foreman's job, a lot of people said you were too young."

"Yeah, but I was twenty-*nine*," he said, "and I'm a *man*."

"What's that got to do with anything?" she asked. "First I can't run the ranch because I'm too young, and now it's because I'm a woman? Which is it, Pete?"

"Both," he replied before he could stop himself.

She pointed a finger at him and said, "Just remember who you work for, Pete Gentry!" She turned and walked up the steps to enter the house.

Gentry watched her until she was gone, then turned and saw that some of the men had been watching and listening to them.

"Get back to work!" he shouted, and the men scattered to find something to do.

Gentry turned again and stared at the closed door

of the house, then kicked the dirt, turned, and stalked off.

O'Grady registered at the hotel which, while not the best hotel in town—according to the liveryman—was suitable for his needs. He got a room overlooking the alley next to the building, then went downstairs to sample the hotel's dining room.

He had a steak and some potatoes, and while the steak was a bit overdone, and the potatoes underdone, the biscuits were good, and the coffee was fine. There were only two other occupied tables in the room, even though it was noon. Obviously this was not one of the more popular eating places in Little Bend.

After lunch he checked to see if the hotel had a bar; it did not, so he left to look for a saloon. When he came to one he decided that instead of going in he'd take one turn around town first, then stop and have a drink. As it happened, the turn around town took a lot longer than he'd expected.

Red Atkins came out of the Lucky Lady Saloon, weaving a bit as he did. It was only two in the afternoon, but already he'd had enough to drink to affect his balance. You couldn't have told him that, however. Quite a few men had absorbed a beating because they tried to tell Red that he was too drunk to drink anymore. While whiskey affected his balance, it also made him mean. A big, hulking man with sloping shoulders and biceps like cannonballs, even drunk he was able to defeat any man in town.

Red decided that he'd had enough to drink—at the Lucky Lady, anyway. He decided to go down the street to the Bull's Eye Saloon and have a few there.

O'Grady had been walking around town for an hour when he came to the Bull's Eye. There were still some streets he hadn't been down, but he decided that he was too thirsty to continue. The saloon was right at hand, so he entered. He was standing at the bar with a beer in hand when Red Atkins barged through the batwing doors.

"Jesus," the bartender said in a low voice. "Red's drunk already."

O'Grady looked at the man, but it was obvious that the bartender was speaking to himself, not to O'Grady, so the redheaded agent turned his attention back to his beer, and to watching the blonde saloon girl.

There were two women working the floor, as it was still too early for the saloon to be full. There were some gaming tables in the place, but they were covered by green cloths and would obviously not be in use until later.

The first woman was dark-haired, in her thirties, and beginning to thicken a bit in the waist. She had very large breasts which were probably not as firm as they had once been. As for her face, she was handsome enough, but not what anyone would call pretty.

The blonde was something else, though. She was tall, willowing, with fuller breasts than you might think when you saw her from behind. Her blonde hair was long, hanging past her shoulders, and her face was very pretty, with an upper and lower lip that were of equal fullness. It gave her the kind of mouth that O'Grady could easily envision biting into—which he was doing now.

Sheriff Cal Festin sat back in his chair and stared at the ceiling. It was the way he spent most of his days. At fifty-five, the days of chasing outlaws cross-country were behind him. He had done that for years as a federal marshal, but now, as the sheriff of Little Bend—a position he had held for the past five years—he looked forward to quiet days and nights. Sure, the town was growing, and things would probably change along the way, but at his age he was looking forward

13

to retirement soon. All he wanted was another year of peace and quiet, and he'd be a happy man.

"Gimme a whiskey," Red said, pounding on the bar.

"Take it easy, Red," the bartender said, but he grabbed a bottle and a glass and poured for the man.

"Don't tell me to take it easy," Red said, grabbing the glass. He downed the whiskey and slammed the glass back down on the bar. "Again."

Red was further down the bar from O'Grady, with several men between them, which suited Canyon just fine. All he wanted was to have a leisurely beer and then get on with his business.

Of course, that was his *intention*, but things never did go the way you planned them, did they?

2

While O'Grady finished his beer, Red Atkins downed another three whiskeys, and while his balance and speech seemed affected, the man did not look as if he was anywhere near falling down.

With each drink he became louder and louder, and men began to leave the bar to get away from him. When the last man moved, he left only Red Atkins and Canyon O'Grady standing at the bar. O'Grady had about one swallow of beer left, and decided to finish it and move on himself.

That was when the blonde came over to him.

"Hello," she said, smiling broadly. In addition to those full lips she had very white teeth, and smooth, pale skin. He found himself looking at the slopes of her breasts, which looked as smooth as glass. "I'm Candy."

"I'll bet you are."

"New in town?"

"Brand new."

"Stayin' long?"

"I guess that depends."

She looked down at his mug and saw that it was empty.

"Want another beer?"

"I only intended to have one."

"Aw, come on, have another one."

"You're not just trying to hustle me into buying another beer, are you?"

"Sweetheart," she said, "I'd be lying if I said I

wasn't. That's my job, after all, and I'd get fired if I didn't do it well." Then she lowered her voice and added, "But let's just say I'm enjoying my job more now than I usually do."

Well, he thought, at least she was honest about it.

"All right, Candy," he said, "I'll have one more beer."

"Bill," she called out, "get the man another beer, will you?"

"You going to stay here while I drink it?" he asked her.

"Honey, I wish I could, but I got other customers here," she said. "But . . ."

"But what?"

"After I get off tonight," she said, putting her hand on his chest, "there's no reason why we can't have a drink together."

"The saloon will be closed then," he said. "Where would we have that drink?"

"You get the bottle," she said, "and I'm sure we can find a place."

The bartender came over and set the full mug of beer in front of O'Grady.

"Come back later," she said, moving closer so that her breasts pressed against his arm. "Don't forget me."

"I couldn't do that," he said.

She turned to walk away from him, passing Red Atkins on the way—only Red wasn't in the mood to let her pass. He reached out, grabbed her arm, and roughly turned her to face him.

"Makin' nice to the new guy, huh, Candy?" Red said. He wrapped one huge arm around her waist and pulled her against him so that his face was right in hers. She turned her face away to try to get away from his foul breath. "How come you never make nice to me like that?"

"Let go of me, Red," she said. She put her hands against his chest and tried to push herself away from him, but he was holding her too tightly.

O'Grady made a face and looked at the bartender, who just shrugged. The red-haired agent knew he should have left after that first beer.

"Come on, Candy," Red said, "make nice to me." He pressed his face against hers and stuck his tongue out.

"Red, cut it out!" she yelled, and now she was beating on him with her fists.

O'Grady put his beer down and closed the distance between himself and Red.

"Okay, friend, let her go."

Red Atkins frowned and looked around, as if he wasn't sure where the voice had come from. Then he saw O'Grady and focused his bleary eyes on him.

"Whacha say?"

"I said let her go!"

"Let 'er go?" Red said. "She don't want me to let 'er go, do ya, honey?"

"Yes, Red, I do," she said. "Let me go right now." And with that she stomped on his foot with her heel. His face turned the color of his name and his mouth opened, although no sound came out. He did release her, though, and she backed away from him, quickly moving out of reach.

"I could have handled him without your help," she said to O'Grady, annoyed.

"I was just trying to help."

"I don't know what your job is, Mister," she said, "but I wouldn't try to tell you how to do it."

O'Grady put his hands up, palms out, and said, "Okay, I'm sorry."

She smiled then, leaned into him, and said, "Don't forget that drink," and then walked away.

O'Grady shook his head and turned. He decided to forget the second beer and just get while the getting

17

was good—only it wasn't. As he started for the door a huge hand landed on his shoulder and turned him around. He saw the big fist coming at him, but couldn't get out of the way in time. The blow caught him on the jaw and he staggered back. Red Atkins was shorter than he was, but he was a good forty pounds heavier, most of it in the upper body.

O'Grady took a half dozen steps back before righting himself; Red Atkins stood his ground with his jaw thrust out.

"Next time mind your own goddamned business!" Red snapped.

O'Grady's first instinct was to wade in and return the blow, but he took a moment to think it over and decided it was not the wise course. He had come to town to do a job, and didn't want to draw too much attention to himself. Also, the other man lived here, and there was no telling how many friends he might have in the saloon.

"Okay, friend," O'Grady said, "you made your point. Why don't you go back to your drinking now and I'll be on my way."

"Oh, no," Atkins said.

"What do you mean, oh, no?" O'Grady said.

"I ain't made my point yet," the other man said. "I ain't made my point until I say I made my point."

"Look, friend," O'Grady said, "what's your name, Red? Look, Red, let's just call it even and forget it, okay? Nothing happened that's worth getting riled over."

"Whataya, yella?" Atkins asked.

"Whatever you say, Red," O'Grady said, and turned to leave.

"Don't turn your back on me!" Red Atkins shouted, and there was something different in his voice that made O'Grady stop. Before it had just been a misunderstanding, and O'Grady had not sensed any urgency about the situation, but suddenly he could sense the danger in the air.

Bill the bartender called over Andy, the swamper, and said, "Go get the sheriff."

"Right."

As the man started away, Bill grabbed him by the arm.

"Go out the back way."

"Right."

Andy went out the back just as O'Grady was turning around. Red Atkins was standing with his arms away from his body. On his right hip he wore a well-worn .45, and looked for all the world like he was about two seconds from drawing it.

"Look, Red," O'Grady said, trying to soothe the other man, "let's not get crazy."

"Crazy?" Red shouted, and the bartender made a face. He remembered what happened to the last man who used that word on Red. "Who's crazy?"

"Nobody," O'Grady said, sensing that he had accidentally pushed the wrong button. Instead of soothing the drunken man, he'd incensed him. "I didn't say anybody—"

"Who are you callin' crazy!" Red shouted, and his face was now turning nearly purple.

O'Grady looked at the bartender, who shrugged much the way he had shrugged earlier when Red had grabbed Candy. O'Grady looked around the saloon at the faces that were watching the action and said, "Does this man have any friends in here?"

"I don't need no friends to take care of you," Red said.

"I mean some friends who might be able to control him?" O'Grady asked.

"Mister," a man seated at a table near him said, "nobody can control Red when he gets like that. Face it: you gotta deal with him yourself."

19

O'Grady took a deep breath, then looked at Red Atkins.

"Okay," O'Grady said, "okay, but no gunplay. There's no need for anybody to get killed."

"I don't need a gun to kill you, friend," Red Atkins said. To illustrate the point he unbuckled his gunbelt and let it drop to the floor. "I'll kill you with my bare hands."

O'Grady unbuckled his own gunbelt, wondering if he was doing the right thing. He was willing to bet that Red Atkins settled most of his differences with his bare hands rather than with a gun. By discarding his own weapon he was stepping right into the man's backyard.

Maybe, just maybe, the man was drunk enough for O'Grady to be able to get this over with relatively fast, with a minimum of damage to property—and to himself.

"Red," the bartender said, "I don't suppose I can get you to take this outside?"

"Forget it, Bill," Red said. "We're gonna settle this right here and now."

"Mister," Bill said, "you wanna pay for your second beer now?"

"Thanks for the vote of confidence," O'Grady said.

"I seen Red fight, Mister," the bartender said. "I ain't never seen you in my life."

"Just leave the beer there," O'Grady said with more bravado than he felt. "I'll pay for it after I finish it."

"You talk big for a tall stringbean," Red Atkins said.

"Come on, Red," O'Grady said, "let's get this over with. I've got other things to do."

"Mister," Red Atkins said, "when I'm done with you, you ain't even gonna be walkin'."

O'Grady looked over at Candy, who chose that moment to blow him a kiss.

Encouragement, he wondered, or was she just kissing him goodbye?

"Come on, friend," Red Atkins said, beckoning O'Grady forward with sausagelike fingers, "come and get your back broken."

3

Red Atkins charged O'Grady immediately, and in doing so surprised the big agent. The man moved quickly for someone his size who was supposed to be drunk. Before O'Grady knew it, he was trapped in a bear hug. He could feel the strength in Atkins's arms and knew that the man did mean to break his back. He had to do something, and quickly.

He strained against the man's hold but was unable to break it. There had to be another way. His arms were pinned inside the bear hug, so there was nothing he could do with them. He had only his head to work with. He reared back and then butted Atkins as hard as he could with his forehead. The man grunted but did not release his hold. O'Grady tried it again, this time butting the man on the bridge of the nose. Atkins roared and released his hold to reach up and grab his nose.

O'Grady, free now, backpedaled away from the man's powerful arms.

"You broke my nose!" Red Atkins shouted. He dropped his hands and O'Grady saw the blood coming from his nose. It covered the lower portion of his face and dripped from his chin.

"I'm gonna kill you!" Atkins shouted, and charged O'Grady again, but this time the agent was ready for him.

O'Grady sidestepped, sticking out his left leg. Atkins tripped over it and slammed into the wall next to the batwing doors. O'Grady was on him immediately.

While the man was stunned he turned him around and hit him in the belly with lefts and rights. He was driving the air from Atkins's lungs, but not doing much damage otherwise. The man was built like a tree trunk.

O'Grady swung Atkins over so that his back was to the doors, then reared back and hit him with a tremendous right hand. The blow caught Atkins flush on the jaw and sent him flying out through the doors in the street.

O'Grady followed him out, and many of the saloon patrons crowded out the doors behind them.

Atkins was lying in the street on his back, stunned, and standing over him was a man wearing a badge. The man turned his head and looked up at O'Grady, who was still standing on the boardwalk. The agent's ribs and back were aching from the short time he had been in the bear hug.

"You responsible for this?" the sheriff asked him.

"I guess you could say that," O'Grady said. "Although he pressed the issue. You can ask anyone, Sheriff. They all saw it. He didn't give me much of a choice."

"Well, knowing Red, I can't say I have any trouble understanding that," the sheriff said. He looked down at Atkins again, who was beginning to get his bearings again. "Okay, Red, let's take a walk to jail."

He leaned over and helped the man to his feet.

"You're takin' *me* to jail?" Red said.

"Just until you sleep it off," the lawman said. He looked up at the crowd in front of the saloon and said, "Where's his gun?"

"I'll get it," someone said. He broke away from the crowd, went inside, and reappeared with Red Atkins's gun, handing it to the sheriff.

The sheriff looked at O'Grady then and said, "Mister, if I was you I wouldn't plan on running into Red when he's sober."

24

"I didn't plan on running into him when he was drunk," O'Grady said. "I'm going to be in town for a few days, Sheriff."

"Well, keep an eye out, then," the lawman said. "He's not likely to forget this."

"He's drunk," O'Grady said. "Maybe he will forget."

"It looks like you busted his nose," the sheriff said. "He's not likely to forget that."

"Thanks for the advice."

"Just trying to avoid more trouble," the sheriff said. "Come on, Red, let's go."

As the sheriff led Atkins away, O'Grady turned to face the crowd of people from the saloon. One man handed him his hat, which had come off during the fight, and someone else handed him his gun.

"Thanks."

"We ain't never seen anybody handle Red like that, Mister," someone said.

"You wanna finish that beer, Mister?" the bartender asked. "It's on the house."

"Mind if I come back for it later?" O'Grady asked.

"Sure, friend, anytime. Jeez, you didn't even break any of my furniture. That's a first with one of Red's fights."

"Glad I could oblige," O'Grady said. "See you later."

A couple of men patted him on the back as he turned to leave and then he walked stiffly away. His ribs and back were aching, and he figured the best thing for them right now was a hot bath.

He hoped his hotel had bathing facilities.

Brenda Edderly sat in her father's office at his desk. Her elbows were on the desk and her head was in her hands. On the desk next to her elbow was a glass of sherry.

The more she thought about it, the more convinced she became that her father had been murdered. She

25

had talked to the sheriff about it, but he had told her she was imagining things. After that she had talked to the judge in town, but he told her the same thing. She'd followed that by riding to the territorial seat to talk with a federal marshal. He told her she needed proof before he could act.

Proof against who? she wondered. She only thought he was murdered, but she had no idea who might have done it. The marshal recommended that she hire a detective, but she had a better idea.

Brenda Edderly had sent some telegrams to Washington, where her father had many friends and many contacts. There were quite a few politicians in office who had gotten there because of her father's money.

As a result of her telegrams, someone was supposed to be coming to help her. She wondered what anyone would be able to do now, two months after her father's death. Even if he was murdered, the trail would have to be cold by now.

She picked up the glass of sherry and drank it down. At least with someone else looking into that end of it she could concentrate on running the ranch. The people around her—like Pete Gentry—may have been right. She might be too young to run the ranch the way her father had run it, but she sure as hell was going to give it a shot. If she found that she couldn't run it, then she'd have to hire someone who could . . . or sell the damned thing.

What did a twenty-three-year-old woman need with a ranch, anyway?

O'Grady soaked in a hot tub at his hotel until the water became tepid, then stepped out and dressed in fresh clothes. He had intended to ride out to the Edderly ranch after his beer, but those plans had certainly gone awry. He was also supposed to send a telegram to his boss in Washington, Major General Rufus Wheeler, and let him know he had arrived.

After that, he was to send another telegram after contact had been made. Wheeler wanted to know if O'Grady thought there was anything to Brenda Edderly's belief that her father had been murdered.

They had talked in his office . . .

"Harlan Edderly had a lot of, uh, contacts in Washington, O'Grady," Wheeler had said. O'Grady had felt at the time that Wheeler had almost used the word "friends," rather than "contacts." "Some of them are putting pressure on us to check out his daughter's suspicions."

"And that's where I come in?" O'Grady asked. "We've gone through this before, General. I'm not a detective—"

"We need someone we can trust, O'Grady," Wheeler had said, "and you certainly fill that bill, don't you?"

"Yes, sir," O'Grady said, "you know I do."

"Uh, the President would like this handled as quickly and quietly as possible, O'Grady. You'll oblige us on that, won't you?"

"I'll do my best, sir."

And his best had gotten him into a bar fight his first day in town. Of course, that wasn't something he'd have to tell General Wheeler in his telegram.

Freshly dressed, O'Grady left the bath facility and stopped at the front desk to ask the clerk where the telegraph office was. Armed with directions, he left the hotel and found the office with no problem. He carefully composed a telegraph message to Wheeler, saying as much as he could in as few words as possible.

When he left the telegraph office it was getting on into early evening, too late to ride out to the Edderly ranch. He'd end up riding back in the dark, and since he was unfamiliar with the territory, that wouldn't be a wise move. He was going to have to wait until morning before he rode out there. Now all he needed to do was decide how he was going to spend his time tonight—at least until his "drink" with Candy. Since he hadn't actually started working yet he didn't see any harm in keeping his date with her. At least that would give him something to do with his night.

"You gotta let me out of here, Sheriff," Red Atkins demanded.

"When you sober up, Red," the lawman said.

Red Atkins tightened his hold on the bars that separated him from the sheriff and said, "I am sober, damn it."

There was a bandage across Atkins's face. The sheriff had allowed the doctor in to examine his nose, which he had pronounced—to no one's surprise—was broken.

"Stay out of fights until it heals, Red," the doctor had said.

"Relax awhile longer, Red," the sheriff said. "Remember what the doctor said."

"I ain't gonna get into another fight," Atkins said.

"Sure, Red, sure," the sheriff said. He had heard that before.

"I ain't, I tell ya," Atkins said. "Let me out of here right now!"

"I'm gonna go out and get you some dinner, Red," the sheriff said. "Maybe after you've eaten I'll let you out."

"Hey," Atkins shouted as the sheriff left. "Hey, come back here!"

O'Grady returned to the hotel to ask the clerk where he could get a decent dinner.

"You've already tried our food here, right?" the man asked.

"Uh, yeah," O'Grady said. "No offense, but—"

"Hey," the man said, "you don't have to explain yourself to me. I don't eat here. There's a little café down on Front Street that serves a delicious beef stew. Go over there. I'm sure you'll enjoy it."

"Okay," O'Grady said, "thanks."

He left the hotel and headed over to Front Street. Beef stew sounded like it would just hit the spot.

4

O'Grady was enjoying the beef stew—which was even better than the desk clerk at the hotel had led him to believe—when the sheriff came walking into the café. The waiter approached him, asking if he wanted to be seated.

"Maybe later, Jerry," the lawman said. "Right now I need some food for my prisoner."

"Prisoner?" Jerry asked. "Anybody I know?"

"Red Atkins."

"Red? Oh, that's right, I heard somebody broke Red's nose today. I'll get you some beef stew for him. Be right back."

As the waiter went into the kitchen, the sheriff noticed O'Grady eating and approached him.

"I see it didn't take you long to find the best eatin' place in town," the sheriff said.

"Is everything here as good as their beef stew?" O'Grady asked.

"Everything is pretty good," the sheriff said. "But the beef stew is their specialty. We didn't get a chance to make proper introductions earlier." The man stuck out his hand and said, "The name's Cal Festin."

"Canyon O'Grady." O'Grady shook the man's hand briefly and then went back to eating. "Is that right?"

"Is what right?" the sheriff asked.

"Did I break Red Atkins's nose?"

"You sure did," the sheriff said. "Gonna make you a minor celebrity in town."

"Not if we don't spread it around," O'Grady said.

31

"That the way you want it?"

"It's the way I'd prefer it, yeah."

"Well, I won't spread it around, but that don't mean it won't get around."

"I'll appreciate whatever you can do, Sheriff."

"Plan on being in town long?"

O'Grady shrugged and said, "A few days, I suppose."

"What's your business?"

O'Grady looked at the sheriff and then said, "That's private, Sheriff—but rest assured I'm not looking for any trouble."

As the waiter came out of the kitchen carrying a covered tray, the sheriff said, "Yeah, I'm sure you weren't looking for trouble this afternoon, either, but it managed to find you."

The sheriff accepted the tray from Jerry and said to O'Grady, "Enjoy the rest of your meal."

"Thanks."

As the sheriff left, O'Grady wondered about Red Atkins, and what would happen when the sheriff finally let him out of jail. Would Atkins make a point of coming after him? Or would the man simply wait until their paths crossed again? And was there any way to avoid having their paths cross again? The last thing O'Grady needed was a drunken—or sober—Red Atkins coming after him.

After he finished dinner he went back to the Bull's Eye Saloon to nurse a couple of beers and wait for Candy to finish work.

After Atkins finished eating his dinner he dropped the tray onto the floor to get Festin's attention.

"Ready to leave?" Festin asked him.

"I was ready a long time ago," Atkins said.

Festin looked closely at Atkins. The hours he had spent in jail, plus the meal he had just finished, had done the trick. If the man wasn't sober, he was damn near, and that was good enough for the sheriff.

"All right, Red," Festin said, inserting the cell key into the lock and unlocking the door, "I'm letting you out, but I don't want any trouble out of you—at least not for a few nights."

"All I wanna do now is get some sleep, Sheriff," Atkins said, stepping out of the cell. "My gun?"

"You need your gun to sleep?" the sheriff asked, but he walked to his desk, opened a drawer and took out the man's gunbelt. "Here."

Atkins took the gunbelt but didn't strap it on. Instead he carried it to the door.

"Remember what I said, Red," Festin said. "No trouble."

"I just need some sleep, Sheriff," Atkins said.

As Atkins went out the door Festin sat behind his desk and crossed his arms. He believed that Atkins was going to go to sleep; it was what he was going to do when he got up that worried him.

5

Poker was just a way to pass the time for Canyon O'Grady. He didn't consider himself a gambler, and yet he enjoyed sitting for a few hours and playing against four or five other men. Although they played for money—sometimes a lot, sometimes very little— poker was not about the money. The money was just the way they kept score.

O'Grady was in the saloon only half an hour, seated at a table alone, when a chair at the poker game going on at the next table opened up. He looked for Candy and saw that she was busily working the floor. He shrugged, picked up his beer and walked over to the table.

"You fellas mind a new player?" he asked.

Four men looked up at him and studied him for a few moments before one of them said, "New blood is always welcome, friend. Pull up a chair."

O'Grady sat down, finished his beer quickly and passed the empty glass to one of the girls passing by.

"Another?" she asked. It was the brunette he had seen earlier that day. Her name was Lori.

"No, thanks," O'Grady said.

Only one of the other players had a drink on the table; the man seated directly across from him had a glass of whiskey at his elbow. He was the only player in the game—other than O'Grady—who was not a citizen of the town. He was dressed in trail clothes, but they were better clothes than you usually saw on a trail hand. O'Grady figured he was a gambler who chose not to dress in the dark, expensive suits that many gamblers wore. O'Grady would also come to realize that the glass of whiskey at the man's elbow was the same glass of whiskey he had purchased when the game began. Occasionally the man picked up his glass and took a small sip, taking in very little liquor, if he took any at all.

The dealer, the man who had invited him to sit, was to O'Grady's right, and made the introductions.

"That's Ed, Paul, and Taylor. I'm Nick."

"O'Grady," the redhaired agent said.

The gambler seated across from him was Taylor. It did not escape him that he and Taylor would be known by their last names, while the other three—who lived in town—were known by their first.

"We play stud and draw, no wild cards, check and raise," the man said. "Minimum bet is ten dollars, and we go on from there."

As games went, it wasn't really a big game, but the hands could vary, depending on how strongly the men felt about their cards.

"Comin' out," the dealer said, "five card stud."

Nick dealt out one card face down, and one face up. O'Grady's card was a ten of hearts. Ed received a five of clubs, Paul a deuce of spades, Taylor a King of diamonds, and Nick dealt himself a three of diamonds. O'Grady's hole card was a King of hearts. He had two hearts and was satisfied to see that there were no other hearts on the table.

"King bets," Nick said to Taylor.

"King bets ten dollars," Taylor said.

O'Grady would discover that there was very little banter at the table, and what there was Taylor never took part in. Taylor studied his cards, and the cards on the table, and the faces of the other players, and only spoke to make his bets.

"Call," Nick said.

"I call," O'Grady said, and so did Ed and Paul.

Ed was Ed King, who owned the general store. Paul Decker owned the hardware store. The dealer, Nick McLish, owned the livery stable, the feed and grain stores, and the gun shop. All three had the money to play poker with a man like Taylor. They were also all on the town council.

"Comin' out," Nick said, and dealt out the third card.

O'Grady got a Queen of hearts. Ed and Paul received low cards out of suit with what they had. Taylor caught another King, this one in spades. Nick got another three, this one in clubs.

"Pair of Kings bets," Nick said.

"Twenty dollars," Taylor said.

Everyone called, and Nick dealt out the fourth card.

O'Grady got another heart, this one a six. He no longer had a chance at a straight flush, but his flush was very much alive. To his consternation Ed caught an eight of hearts, but no other hearts appeared on the table. Paul caught a card that was mismatched with the other two. Taylor caught an Ace of diamonds, and the hand became interesting when Nick dealt himself a third three.

"Three threes," Nick said, almost sheepishly.

"It's a good thing we know you, Nick," Ed said, "or we'd be wonderin'."

"Yeah," Paul said, smiling, "it's a good thing we know you're all thumbs."

He looked at Taylor, still smiling, but when the man did not return the smile Paul dropped his and looked away nervously.

"Uh, well, three of a kind, even this small, is worth fifty dollars."

O'Grady stayed, even though he knew that if Nick caught another pair and he caught his flush, he would lose. Ed and Paul folded, but Taylor stayed.

"Last card," Nick said, and dealt it.

O'Grady received a five of hearts. He had his flush.

37

Taylor got another Ace. He now had Kings and Aces on the table.

Nick dealt himself a Jack of spades. He now had three of a kind and the Jack on the table. If he had another Jack underneath—or a fourth three—he was a winner.

Of course, if he had another Jack and Taylor also filled up, he'd lose. Either way, O'Grady would be last man on the totem pole, even with a flush.

Of course, O'Grady knew he had his flush, and had to bet it to find out what the others had.

"Three threes bets a hundred," Nick said.

Of course he had to get a hundred. He was high on board. Not to bet would be telling O'Grady and Taylor that all he had was the three threes.

O'Grady hesitated just a moment, then said, "Your hundred," throwing the money into the pot, "and another hundred."

When O'Grady sat down he hadn't realized that the very first hand would turn into hundred dollar bets. If he lost this hand he was going to have to embarrass himeslf by leaving the game. He had more money, but it was hidden in his saddle. He only had about another two hundred dollars on him. This—along with what he had in his saddle—was his expense money, and he couldn't afford to lose it all.

Taylor studied O'Grady while the agent and Nick waited. O'Grady had a King in the hole, so Taylor had three chances to make his full house. He could have the case king, or another Ace in the hole. If he bet, O'Grady was going to fold. The man was looking at two potentially powerful hands and would be foolish to try and bluff. One of the other players would surely call him. O'Grady didn't think Taylor would bluff. If he bet he had it. If he didn't have it, he would fold.

"I fold," Taylor said, and turned over his cards.

"Ha!" Nick said. "I was worried about you, Taylor." He looked at O'Grady and said, "I call your hundred and raise a hundred. I don't think you have your flush, O'Grady."

Now O'Grady knew he was a winner. By announcing that he didn't think O'Grady had his flush Nick was telling the table that he had not filled in his hand. He only had three threes, and was betting that he had the winning hand.

"Your hundred, and another," O'Grady said. Now if he lost he'd really have to leave—but he didn't think he was going to lose. If Nick was smart he'd fold, but on the other hand he wasn't going to do that without looking at O'Grady's hole card.

Nick frowned, compressed his lips and then said, "All right, I call. Let's see the flush."

O'Grady tossed his King of hearts on top of Nick's three threes.

"Flush," Taylor said. "A winner. Well played, O'Grady."

"Shit," Nick said, flipping over his hole card, which was a useless nine of hearts.

"You deal," Taylor said to O'Grady as the agent raked his pot in.

"Same game," O'Grady said, shuffling and then dealing.

6

"I'm ready," Candy said to O'Grady. She had leaned over and spoken into his ear between hands. "When you are, that is."

He turned his head and looked at her.

"The place doesn't look like it's ready to close," he said.

"It's not," she said, putting her hand on his shoulder. "It's just that I'm ready."

"Give me ten minutes," he said, and she nodded and moved away.

"One more hand, fellas," O'Grady said. "I've got a lady waiting for me."

"Gonna pay her with our money, too," Ed King said, sourly.

O'Grady had been doing very well. He and Taylor had won all of the money between them, while the three town fathers had done all the losing. In Taylor's case his skill was keeping him ahead. As far as O'Grady was concerned, he had never been as lucky as he was that night. He didn't know how much money he had won during the two hours he had played, but it had to be over a thousand dollars.

Taylor dealt out the last hand, which O'Grady stayed in to the end, looking for a flush. When it didn't come, he folded. As it happened, Ed King won the hand.

"Gentlemen," O'Grady said, standing up.

"Sure," King said, "quit when I start to get hot."

O'Grady ignored the man's comment.

"Maybe another time," he said, and he was looking at Taylor.

"I look forward to it, Mr. O'Grady," Taylor said. "Your presence in the game was very enjoyable."

"Thanks," O'Grady said.

He turned and walked to the bar, where Candy was waiting for him with a bottle of whiskey.

"Ready?" he asked.

"I sure am," she said . . .

. . . and she was. She was so ready that she was all over him before he could even close the door of his room. Her mouth was on his and her hands were everywhere, undoing his gunbelt and dropping it to the floor, unbuttoning his shirt, opening his pants, and then allowing him to return the favor. He unfastened her dress from behind and it fell away from her. She wore nothing underneath, which delighted him. Her breasts were full and her flesh was as smooth as it had looked. Luckily, it wasn't as cold as glass is. It was hot and firm and pliant beneath his hands, and he lifted her breasts to his mouth and bit her nipples. She gasped and clasped his head to her. He sucked her nipple and slid one hand down between her legs, finding her wet and very ready—as promised.

She was strong and steered him to the bed. When the back of his legs struck the mattress he fell onto it, with her on top. She crawled all over him, her mouth avidly tasting him. She licked his nipples and kissed her way down to his navel, which she lingered over lovingly with her tongue. She then moved still further down, leaving a wet trail until she reached his rigid penis.

"Oh, God . . ." she breathed, "it's so beautiful . . . it's so hot . . . it's so . . . ." She didn't go on because by this time it was in her mouth. She was sucking him like a piece of hard candy, cupping his testicles in her hands like a couple of fragile jewels.

"Mmmm . . ." she moaned with her mouth full. "Oh . . ." she groaned around him, and then her head went all the way down on him and he felt as if her mouth were sucking him in completely . . . and he exploded, almost without warning. It was the oddest orgasm he'd ever had. Usually he knew when he was about to climax, but this . . . this was something special. This girl had a mouth that was like magic, and she used it on him again . . . and again . . . as the night went on . . . and on . . . and on. . . .

In the morning a shaft of sunlight shot through the window and struck O'Grady in the face. He awoke and everything was red behind his eyelids. He cracked his eyes open slowly, then turned his head right and left to get away from the sun. When that didn't work he lifted his hand to shade his eyes, and that worked . . . for the time being.

Something warm was next to him—no, that was some*one* warm, and he turned his head to look. He saw some tousled blonde hair on a pillow, but the face was hidden beneath the blanket. So was the body, but he could feel that against his own underneath the sheet. It was smooth and extremely hot and he was suddenly aware of the fact that he had a huge, raging erection. He awoke some mornings like that, and it was usually taken care of by a simple biological function, but this morning he didn't think that function was going to be enough.

He sat up and slowly peeled the sheet and blanket away from the blonde head. First her face came into view, then her breasts, its pink nipples soft . . . then her waist, with no hint of slack flesh, even in repose . . . then the hips . . . and then her long, slender legs . . .

"Mmm," she said, but she was still asleep. She rolled onto her back, and her breasts flattened against her chest. She moved her legs and they opened, bring-

43

ing her sex into view. It was pink, surrounded by downy blonde hair, and it was moist, even early in the morning. It struck him that a woman like Candy was probably always ready. Not that she was a saloon girl, that wasn't what he meant. It's just that she was obviously a gal who loved sex. He remembered everything that happened during the night, and he knew that she loved sex. Every second they were together she was making noises, happy and pleased noises, and was obviously enjoying herself immensely—as he had.

He stared at her moist sex and then reached out to spread her knees just a bit more. He slid between her legs, pressed the spongy head of his erect penis against her wet portal and then . . . plunged.

"Oh God!" she cried out, coming awake. She closed her legs on him and wrapped her arms around him and began moving her hips. "Oh, Jesus, Canyon O'Grady!" she said, as if she wanted to be sure that he knew that she knew who he was. "Oooh, Jesus, God, what a way to wake up!"

He began to slam into her, almost mindless in his pursuit of orgasm this morning. It was as if nothing existed for him from the waist up—except for those firm breasts which were crushed beneath him, and her moist mouth, which was first on his neck, then his face, and then fastened to his mouth. She continued to moan and even speak into his mouth as they slammed into each other, both wanting the same thing and neither having any intention of stopping until they both got it . . .

"My God," she said later, pushing her hair away from her face with one hand, "I can't remember the last time I had a night—and a morning—like that. . . . In fact, I can't remember ever having a night *and* a morning like that, together."

"I'll take that as a compliment," he said, lying beside her.

"Mmmm," she said, sliding her hand down over his belly until she was holding his semi-erect penis in her hand. "Canyon O'Grady, you are a woman's man."

"What's that mean?"

"You know how to satisfy a woman," she said. "That's rare in a man. Most men only know how to take their own pleasure. I count myself lucky to have found a man who wanted me to be as happy as he was."

"I'm sorry," he said, "but a woman's enjoyment is important to me. For one thing, you wouldn't want to come back up here if you didn't enjoy it, would you?"

"Don't apologize, Mr. O'Grady," she said, sliding her hand up and down the length of him. "Don't apologize to me, honey."

He looked down at her hand and said, "If you're hoping for something else to happen this morning, I think you'd better give up."

"Is that so?" she asked, looking down at him as well. She looked at his face then and said, "You know, I think I'll take that as a challenge."

"Candy—" he said, but she shimmied down and began working on him with her tongue and her magic mouth and damned if he didn't start to rise to the challenge himself.

Candy left before O'Grady did, pleading a need for her "beauty" sleep. O'Grady remained in bed for a few minutes, enjoying the warmth she had left behind, inhaling her fragrance, and the fragrance of their sex, and then rising and washing with a pitcher and bowl the hotel provided. After that he dressed and went downstairs for breakfast.

At breakfast he planned his day. Immediately following the meal he would walk to the livery to retrieve

Cormac and would then ride out to the ranch to talk with Brenda Edderly about her father's death. He really didn't see all that much he'd be able to do. Even if the man was murdered, that was two months ago. What were the chances that he'd be able to pick up a murderer's trail after all that time? As he had told Wheeler again and again for years—not that it did much good—he really wasn't a detective. Still, he'd promised to do his best, and that was the least he could do just to earn the salary he was drawing from the United States Government.

When Brenda Edderly awoke that morning she laid in bed awake, her arms folded across her breasts. She'd had an erotic dream, and was trying to remember it at the same time she was waiting for it to fade. At twenty-three she had a healthy appetite for sex. Before her father's death she had occasionally spent a night with Peter Gentry, but since then she had refused to allow him into her bed. After all, he was now working for her, and what kind of business relationship would they have if she was letting him sleep with her?

On mornings like this, though, she could feel her resolve weakening. She slid one hand down over her belly and underneath her gown. With the other hand she cupped first one firm breast, and then the other. Her nipples were hard, and she was wet. What she needed, she guessed, was to find another man who could fill that need for her. However, she had settled on Gentry originally because the pickings in Little Bend were pretty slim to begin with.

Finally, she rose and decided to take a bath—a cold one!

As he left the hotel, it occurred to O'Grady to look both ways for Red Atkins. He didn't believe that the man was the type to just forget what had happened between them. Drunk or sober, the next time he saw the man he was going to have to be prepared to deal with him.

He walked to the livery, saddled Cormac, got directions to the ranch from the liveryman, and rode out.

7

O'Grady was impressed with the Edderly Ranch. He passed markers identifying the land, and it was still better than an hour before he came within sight of the main house. It was a huge two story structure, surrounded by smaller buildings such as the bunkhouse, two barns and other buildings he couldn't readily identify the purpose of.

As he rode up to the main house he was the center of attention. There was a lot of activity around the house and the corral, and most of it stopped when he went by. He felt as if he was on display.

As he dismounted, a single man broke away from the others and approached him, removing gloves as he came. The man was in his early thirties, a serious looking man with good shoulders and breadth of chest. A hard worker, O'Grady figured, and from the look on his face and the way he carried himself, someone in authority.

"Can I help you?" the man asked him.

"Yes," O'Grady said, "I'd like to see Miss Brenda Edderly."

"What's your business with her?"

"My name is Canyon O'Grady."

The man waited a beat, then said, "That don't tell me what your business is."

"I think that's between me and Miss Edderly," O'Grady said. "Don't you?"

The man studied him for a moment, slapping the

gloves he held in his left hand into his right palm. He stopped then and pointed at O'Grady.

"You're the detective she sent for."

Since no one was to know that O'Grady worked for the government, he assumed that this was the story Miss Edderly had spread.

"Could you tell her I'm here, please?" he said. He tried to sound polite, but even to his own ears it sounded condescending.

The man's back straightened and he said, "My name's Pete Gentry. I'm the foreman here."

"Glad to meet you," O'Grady said, and waited.

Gentry studied him critically for a few moments, then finally said, "Wait here. I'll tell Miss Edderly that you're here."

"Thank you."

Gentry went up the steps to the front door and entered the house without knocking. One of the advantages of being the foreman, O'Grady guessed. He waited about ten minutes, suffering the scrutiny of the ranch hands without acknowledging them, holding Cormac's reins in his hands. Finally, Gentry reappeared and came back down the steps. The man waved at someone, and another man approached.

"Give your horse to Adams and follow me. Miss Edderly will see you in her father's office."

O'Grady handed over the reins and this time when Gentry went up the steps, he followed him. Gentry opened the front door, entered, waited for O'Grady to enter, then closed the door and led the way again, this time down a hallway. It occurred to O'Grady to ask Gentry why the office was still her father's and not hers, now that her father was dead. He decided not to bring it up, since he didn't know the relationships involved.

Seated behind a desk in the office was a very attractive woman in her early to mid-twenties. She had long, tawny colored hair and an amazing pair of eyes. They were an unremarkable brown, but what made them so amazing was the shape of them. They were almond shaped, although there was no trace of Oriental in the woman's features. Rather than Oriental, they were cat's eyes, and he liked them very much. They went very well with her high cheekbones and full mouth.

"Mr. O'Grady?" she asked.

"That's right."

She looked at the foreman and said, "That's all, Pete."

"Don't you want me to—"

"Close the door on your way out, please?" she said, cutting him off.

O'Grady didn't look at the man, but he could sense his displeasure. He waited until he heard the door close, then approached the desk. Brenda Edderly didn't rise, but she extended her hand and he shook it. It was all very businesslike.

"Please, have a seat," she said. "Thank you for coming."

"I don't know what I can do for you, Miss Edderly," he said. "But why don't we start with you telling me what happened to your father?"

"It's very simple," she said. "He died from a blow to the head."

"How did he receive that blow to the head?"

"Well," she said, "the sheriff says he was out riding, fell off his horse and struck his head on a rock. The doctor says he died instantly from it."

"And you don't believe it?"

"No," she said, "I don't. My father was too good a horseman for that to have happened."

"Is it possible that the horse threw him?"

"No," she said. "Dad had been riding Samson for fifteen years, Mr. O'Grady. I don't think old Sam would have had the energy to throw Dad off, even if he wasn't such a good rider."

"How old was your father?"

"Sixty-three," she said, "but unlike Samson, my father was still a robust man. You only have to ask some of the women in town about that."

"Was he seeing some women in town?"

"Yes," she said, "he was seeing them."

Her tone made it clear that her father was not only seeing them, but was enjoying them in the biblical sense, as well.

"So you think your father was murdered?"

"I don't think he died accidentally," she said, "and he certainly wouldn't kill himself that way. What does that leave?"

"Do you know anyone with a motive for killing your father?"

"Almost anyone he did business with," she said. "He was a ruthless businessman."

"What about the women he was, uh, seeing."

"What about them?"

"Were any of them married?"

"I don't believe so," she said. "Amy Ivy is a widow, Mary Chaplin is in her forties, but she's never been married."

"Were all of the women younger than your father?"

"Oh, yes," she said. "He had no interest in women his own age. As a matter of fact, Amy Ivy is barely older than I am."

"Did you object to that?"

She frowned and said, "Are you suggesting I killed my own father because I didn't approve of one of his bedmates, Mr. O'Grady?"

"I wasn't suggesting anything, Miss Edderly," he said. "That question was just one of curiosity."

"Well, to satisfy any further curiosity," she said, "I did not disapprove of any of my father's friends. Who his friends were or weren't was his business. He felt the same way about me."

O'Grady scratched his head and said, "All right. I'd like to see where the incident happened."

"I'll take you out there myself," she said, standing up. "Do you have any other questions before we leave?"

"I'll probably have some more once we get out there," he said.

"Very well," she said. "Let's go outside and I'll have my horse saddled."

As he followed her outside he was very pleased that the rest of her looked as good as her face did. She was a big woman, tall and full-bodied, made even taller by the boots that she was wearing.

He didn't bother telling her that he couldn't think of any more questions, and was going to use the ride to try and come up with some.

Brenda Edderly's horse was a pretty but powerfully built bay mare about four years old. The animal fit its rider to a T. O'Grady followed her out to the spot where her father was found by two ranch hands who were returning from a day's work.

O'Grady dismounted to take a look around. They hadn't spoken on the way out, but she was talking now.

"The doctor said he probably was out here all day, but that he had most likely died as soon as his head hit that rock."

"This rock?"

"Yes," she said. "I thought about moving it, but . . ."

O'Grady knelt by the rock. It was big, the size of a good water bucket, only it was round. There was a splash of red which he was sure was her father's blood. Of course, just because there was blood on the rock didn't mean that her father had necessarily hit his head there. If he was killed, the blood could have been applied to the rock to be consistent with the story of the accident.

"Who were the two men who found him?" he asked.

"Just a couple of hands."

"What were their names?"

"You wouldn't know them."

He stood up and looked at her.

"I'll get to know them, Miss Edderly."

"Gorman Dwyer and Hannibal Dundee."

O'Grady nodded, filing the men's names away for future reference.

"How long have they worked here?"

"I don't know for sure," she said. "About two or three years, I guess."

"Hired by your father?"

"No," she said, "they would have been hired by Pete."

"That's Pete Gentry, your foreman."

"Yes, that's right."

"Was he in the habit of hiring men without your father's approval?"

"He was the foreman," she said. "He had the right to do so."

O'Grady felt that she dwelled ever so slightly on the word "had," and that this had more to do with the fact that her father was dead. He had the feeling that Pete Gentry was not going to have the same power under the daughter that he had under the father.

"All right," he said. He mounted up and used that vantage point to take a look at the surrounding countryside. "I'm finished here."

"Will you stay, Mr. O'Grady?" she asked. "Will you look into my father's death?"

He really didn't have enough information to make a call on whether her father had been killed or died accidentally, but he decided to stick around and ask some more questions. He wanted to talk to the foreman, the two men who found the body, the sheriff, and the doctor. After that, if he felt there was no evidence of foul play, he'd say so and leave. Meanwhile . . .

"I'll stay awhile, Miss Edderly," he said. "Long enough to ask a few more questions, anyway. . . ."

8

When they got back to the ranch, Brenda Edderly offered O'Grady the hospitality of her home. He didn't feel that her heart was in it, but that had nothing to do with his refusal.

"I don't think that would be a good idea, Miss Edderly," he said, looking down at her. She had dismounted, and he had not. "I have a room at a hotel in town. I think I'll just stay there."

"Whatever you say," she said. "What will you be doing first?"

"Asking questions," he said. "I'll get back to town and get right to it."

"I appreciate this, Mr. O'Grady," she said. "Your willingness to help, I mean. The others . . . well, they just patted me on the head and told me I was imagining things."

"You may be imagining things, Miss Edderly," O'Grady said. "But I didn't come all this way just to pat you on the head and tell you that. I'll be in touch."

"I'll be waiting to hear what you find out."

"It may be nothing," he warned her.

"I'm aware of that," she said. "I'll still be waiting."

He touched the brim of his hat and said, "It shouldn't be more than a few days before I have something to tell you."

She nodded, and he turned his horse and rode out. He realized that he was just as much the center of attention riding out as he had been riding in—maybe even more so.

As O'Grady rode out, Brenda Edderly turned and found a ranch hand walking toward her.

"I'll take the bay, Miss Edderly."

She tried to remember his name, and did. "Thank you, Jerry."

The man took the mare and started walking it to the large barn. Brenda was going up the steps when she heard footsteps behind her. When she reached the top she turned to look and saw Pete Gentry coming toward her.

"Brenda," he called, mounting the steps, "I want to talk to you."

"About what, Pete?"

"About this detective you've hired," he said, coming level with her on the porch.

"What about him?"

"Well, I don't think it's a good idea."

"I didn't ask you," she said. "But why not?"

"I just don't, that's all."

"Well," she said, turning and walking to the door, "I'm glad you have a good reason."

"Brenda—"

"I'm tired, Pete," she said. "I'm going to rest a bit and then I'll be in my father's—I'll be in the office. If you want to talk about ranch business, we'll do it there."

"I don't only want to talk about ranch business, damn it!" he snapped.

She looked at him and said, "I don't really think we have anything else to talk about, Pete." She went inside and closed the door, leaving Gentry standing there, fuming.

He turned abruptly to see if any of the men were looking his way, but they had all turned their head just in time.

Slowly he went back down the steps, trying not to show how angry he was. What did she mean, treating him that way? Who did she think she was? Who did she think he was? Wait, he thought, just wait until she had to come to him and ask him for help. He'd make her grovel, he'd make her plead, he . . . he wouldn't do any of those things. He'd help her, and be glad that she had finally come to him.

Damned women!

When O'Grady got back to town he left Cormac at the livery and went to the saloon for a cold beer. When he walked in he saw Candy working the floor. She smiled at him and he nodded and walked to the bar.

"Hello, Mr. O'Grady," the bartender said. "Decide to stay in town awhile?"

"A few days, Bill," O'Grady said. "How about a cold beer?"

"Comin' up," the man said. He drew the beer and put it down in front of O'Grady. "Those boys you were playin' poker with will sure be glad to hear that you're stayin'."

"Oh? Why's that?"

"Give them a chance to get their money back," Bill said. "They all lost to that gambler, Taylor, after you left last night."

"They're not very good poker players, Bill," O'Grady said. "I mean, I'm not very good and I managed to beat them."

"That ain't what I heard."

O'Grady put the beer mug down half-empty and asked, "What did you hear?"

"That fella, Taylor? He said afterward that you were a damned good poker player."

"Well," O'Grady said, reaching for the mug again," he was probably comparing me to those other three."

"Anyway, I'm glad you're stayin'," Bill said. "But was I you, I'd be on the lookout for Red Atkins."

Damn, O'Grady thought. He'd actually forgotten about Atkins.

"I'll do that," O'Grady said.

As Bill walked down the bar to serve other customers, Candy came walking over to O'Grady.

"Get your business done?" she asked.

"Not quite," he said. "Seems like I'll be here another couple of days, at least."

"My, my," she said, "I don't know if I'll be able to survive that. You could give a woman enough pleasure in two days to kill her."

"Well," he said, "we can put that to the test starting tonight."

"I'm working later tonight."

"I'll be awake," he said. He finished his beer and put the empty mug down. "I'll be back later."

"I'll be waiting," she promised.

He smiled at her, touched the brim of his hat, and walked out.

O'Grady's first stop was the sheriff's office. Festin looked up as the redheaded agent entered, and sat back in his chair, folding his hands in his lap.

"Red ain't here," he said. "I cut him loose last night."

"I'm not here about Red."

"Best news I heard all day," Festin said. "What are you here for?"

"I want to talk about Harlan Edderly."

"Harlan Edderly?" Festin said, frowning. "What do you want to talk about him for? He's dead. Been dead the better part of two months."

"That's what I want to talk about," O'Grady said. "How he died."

"He fell off his horse and hit his head," Festin said.

"Could happen to anybody. That what your business is here? You a dectective or somethin'?"

"Or something," O'Grady said. "Miss Edderly had asked me to look into the death of her father."

"Why? She don't still believe that somebody killed him, does she?"

"Let's just say that she's not really satisfied that her father fell off his horse. She says he was too good a horseman for that."

"Like I said," Festin said, fidgeting in his chair, "it could happen to anybody."

"I know that," O'Grady said.

"Then what are you askin' so many questions for?" Festin said.

"That's what I do best, Sheriff," O'Grady said. "Ask questions. When did you get called onto the scene?"

"Ranch hand came to town to fetch me and the doctor. We rode out there together."

"Where was the body when you got there?"

"Lying on the ground."

"Where?"

"Whataya mean, 'where'? Where it fell, that's where. On the ground."

"Near the rock?"

"What rock?"

"The one everybody says he hit his head on."

"He did hit his head," Festin said. "There was blood on . . . the . . . rock." He punctuated each of the last three words by pointing his finger at O'Grady.

"Yes, I know," the agent said, "I saw the blood."

"Well, there," Festin said. "You saw it yourself."

"Is that all you saw? The blood?"

"What else was there to see?"

"The position of the body."

Festin looked annoyed. He leaned forward in his chair and rested his elbows on his desk.

"I ain't no damned detective," he said. "What the

61

hell do I know about the position of the body? He was lyin' on the ground with his head near the rock."

"Near the rock," O'Grady said. "Not on it?"

"On it, near it, what's the difference?" Festin said. "The doc says he hit his head on the rock and died."

"What's the doctor's name?"

"Green," Festin said, "Marty—Martin Green."

"Is he the only doctor in town?"

"Yep."

"Where can I find him?"

"In his office, most likely," the sheriff said. "Up the block just a few doorways. That was why we got out there so fast, on account of our offices are so close together and they didn't have to go lookin' for either of us."

"Uh-huh," O'Grady said. "Okay, Sheriff. Thanks for talking to me."

"You gonna talk to him now?"

"That was my plan, yeah," O'Grady said. "Any reason why I shouldn't?"

"No," Festin said, his tone noncommittal, "no, no reason."

"Thanks again, Sheriff," O'Grady said, and left the man's office.

After he was gone the sheriff sat back in his chair again, shaking his head. Damn fool woman had gone and brought in some outsider busybody who was gonna cause trouble, see if he didn't. Maybe the best thing would have been if Red Atkins had gone and killed the man yesterday.

9

O'Grady might have asked Festin more questions about the doctor, but that would have given him some preconceived notions about the man. He decided to leave the impression that the doctor would make up to the doctor himself.

He walked up the street, and three doors away found a shingle on the wall that read: Martin Green, M.D. Come Right In.

He opened the door and found himself in what appeared to be a small, empty waiting room. At that moment, a connecting door opened and a man stepped out, ushering an old woman out ahead of him.

"Now, don't worry about it, Mrs. Fletcher," the doctor was saying. "You're going to be just fine."

"I hope so," she said. "If I die, who'll take care of my mister?"

"Don't worry," the doctor said again, "you'll be taking care of your mister for a long time to come."

The doctor kept talking to her until he finally—and gently—pushed her out the front door.

When the man turned, he and O'Grady examined each other. The doctor was tall, with short, gray hair and a wide jaw. He wore wire-framed glasses and looked to be in his mid-forties. He was slender except for his belly, which was too big for a man who was as thin as he was everywhere else.

"You look healthy enough," he said to O'Grady. "What's wrong with you?"

"Nothing."

"Then why are you here?"

"You're Dr. Green, aren't you?"

"That's right."

"I'm here to talk about Harlan Edderly."

"Mr. Edderly?" Green said, frowning. "He's dead. He's been dead for months."

"I know," O'Grady said. "It's how he died I'm interested in."

"What do you mean, how?"

"By accident . . . or by design."

Green frowned and said, "Are you working for Brenda Edderly?"

"That's right."

"And she still thinks her father was murdered?"

"She's just not sure that he died the way you say he did, Doctor. It was you who said he died accidentally, wasn't it?"

"That's right," Green said, then backstepped a bit and said, "that's the way it looked."

"You mean, that's the way it obviously looked," O'Grady said. "What if you had looked a little . . . deeper?"

"Deeper? I don't know what you mean."

"What if you hadn't been so convinced that the death was accidental?" O'Grady asked. "Would you have looked further? For something else?"

"There was nothing else," Green said. "The man fell off his horse and hit his head."

"Okay," O'Grady said, "try this. Mr. Edderly died as the result of a blow to the head, right?"

"That's right."

"What if someone struck him from behind," O'Grady said, "and then laid him out next to that rock?"

"There was blood on the rock."

"It could have been put there," O'Grady said.

"But why?"

"I don't know."

"Then why are you bringing it up?"

"Just as another possibility," O'Grady said. "That is a possibility, isn't it, Doctor?"

"I don't see—"

"I'm just asking if that's a possibility."

The doctor hesitated and then said. "Well, anything's possible."

"Ah," O'Grady said. "See? You do have an open mind. Now, if someone struck him—where was he hit?"

"He hit the back of his head."

"All right," O'Grady said, "if he was struck from behind that means that someone was there with him. There would have been tracks from another horse. Did you happen to notice—"

"There could have been a dozen horses there," the doctor said. "In fact, by the time we got there, there was almost a dozen people there. I couldn't have told anything from the ground, and I'm not a trained . . . what is it? Sign reader?"

"That's right."

"Perhaps you should ask someone else who was there what they saw," Dr. Green said. "I saw a man who had fallen off his horse, struck his head and died. Now if you'll excuse me, I have another patient coming in soon."

"All right, Doctor," O'Grady said, "I'll leave you to your patient . . . but we'll talk again, soon."

O'Grady turned and left, closing the door behind him. The doctor stood there a few moments, staring at the closed door, then turned and went into his examining room. He did have one more patient to see that he knew of. After that, he was going to go and talk to the sheriff about this fella . . . Jesus, he hadn't even asked the man his name!

After O'Grady left the doctor he decided to stop at the local newspaper office. As he stepped inside he was assailed by the smell of ink and the sound of a printing press. He waited for the noise to stop before calling out to announce himself.

A man with ink smudges on his face, arms, and clothes turned and stared at him myopically from behind a pair of thick glasses.

"Can I help you?"

"Are you the editor?"

"Editor, owner, printer, reporter," the man said. "Everything. How can I help you?"

"I'd like to look at some back issues of your newspaper," O'Grady said.

"Which ones? How far back?"

"Two months, I think," O'Grady said. "I want to read whatever you wrote about the death of Harlan Edderly."

"What I wrote—well, I could probably tell you what I wrote, but yeah, you can read it. I'll get the papers for you. Wait here."

O'Grady waited while the man went into another room. When he returned he was well burdened with newspapers. As he put them down he was surprised by the look on O'Grady's face.

"Oh, we ran with this story for a couple of weeks," the man explained. "Also, you know when the daughter started talking about murder? I did some stuff on that, too."

"My name is O'Grady," the agent said.

"Stilwell," the other man said, "Steve Stilwell." Stilwell was in his early forties, about five nine and very slender. He had several days' growth of stubble on his face, and dark hair that was showing just a hint of gray.

"Mr. Stilwell, I'm interested in what Miss Edderly has said about her father's death."

"That it wasn't an accident?"

"Exactly. What do you think about that?"

"Well," Stilwell said, "Harlan Edderly certainly had enough enemies, Mr. O'Grady. I don't find it hard to believe that someone might have wanted to kill him."

"Do you think he was killed?"

Stilwell smiled and shrugged helplessly.

"I wasn't at the scene, Mr. O'Grady. I don't have enough facts to make a statement either way. Why don't you read what I wrote about it in the paper, and then we can talk later. I've still got some work to do."

"All right," O'Grady said. "I appreciate your help."

"I'm not helping just for the sake of helping," Stilwell said. "If you find out something, I'd like to know about it."

"If I find out something," O'Grady said, "you'll hear about it, don't worry—after I've told Miss Edderly."

"You're working for her, then?"

"Let's say I'm working on her behalf."

"Uh-huh," Stilwell said. "You're one of those, huh?"

"One of what?"

"One of those people who don't answer a question directly. Never mind, don't deny it. Just read and then we'll talk."

Stilwell went back to his printing press while O'Grady started going through the newspapers.

It took O'Grady the better part of an hour to go through the various articles, and by the time he was done his hands were black from ink and dust.

Stilwell came over as O'Grady was gathering together the newspapers.

"What did you find out?" the newspaperman asked.

"Not much more than I knew already," O'Grady said, shaking his head.

"Well, all I knew and could write was what people told me."

"You never speculated about who might have killed him—if he'd been killed, I mean."

Stilwell shrugged helplessly and said, "If I'd had even an inkling of such a thing I would have speculated from here to gone, but nobody mentioned it . . . until Brenda did, that is."

"How well do you know Miss Edderly?" O'Grady asked.

"Pretty well," Stilwell said. "I came here ten years ago, when she was just becoming a young woman. She's quite a girl, really."

"Do you think she'll be able to run the ranch?"

"Well now," Stilwell said, rubbing his jaw and leaving a fresh ink smudge, "a lot of people around here don't think so, but I tell you what. If she wants to—and that's a big if—she'll do just fine."

"You think that maybe she won't want to run it?"

"I think a twenty-three-year-old girl—or woman—can find plenty of other things she'd rather do, don't you?"

O'Grady agreed.

"Thanks for your help, Mr. Stilwell," he said, sticking out his hand.

"My pleasure, Mr. O'Grady," Stilwell said. "You, uh, wouldn't want to tell me who you are and what your interest is, would you?"

"My name is Canyon O'Grady and my interest is in seeing whether or not Brenda Edderly is right about her father being killed."

"And I could print that," Stilwell said, "and not much else?"

O'Grady shrugged and said, "That's about all I can tell you, right now."

"I accept that," Stilwell said. "If there's anything

else you want to tell me along the way, don't hesitate, okay?"

"Sure," O'Grady said. "Thanks again."

He left the newspaper office and went back to the hotel to wash the dust and ink off himself.

10

While O'Grady was in the newspaper office, Dr. Green finished with his patient and left his office. He hurried along the boardwalk to the sheriff's office and entered in an agitated state. Festin looked up quickly as the physician entered his office and closed the door tightly behind him.

"That fella O'Grady came to see me, Cal," he said.

"I know," Festin said. "I figured he would."

"What are we gonna do?" Green asked.

"Nothing."

"What do you mean, nothing?"

"He's not gonna find out anything, Marty," Festin said, "so there's no need for us to do anything, is there?"

"But what if he does find out something?"

"And who's gonna tell him?"

"I don't know!" Green shot back. "Somebody!"

"Nobody that wants to keep livin' in this town, that's for sure," Festin said.

"Cal, we've got to do something."

Festin got up, walked around the desk and grasped the doctor's arm in a painful grip.

"You got to get a hold of yourself, Marty," the lawman said. "We only got each other to depend on, you know."

"What about the others?"

"I'll talk to the others," Festin said, releasing the man's arm, "and if anything has to be done, Marty, I'll take care of it. Don't worry."

"Sure," Green said, "that's easy to say. 'Don't worry.' "

"Go back to your office, have a drink, and see some more patients," Festin said. "That's about all you can do, right now."

"Yeah, okay," Green said, nodding, "I'll do that." He started for the door, but turned before he reached it. "You keep me informed, Cal."

"You'll know everything I do, Marty."

Green stared at him, and then said, "Well, I don't know if I want to know all that much . . ." and left.

Sheriff Festin went back around his desk to sit down, wondering where Red Atkins might be at that very moment.

After O'Grady had cleaned up, he left the hotel once again and decided it was time to get something to eat. Over a steak and some potatoes at a small café he went over what he had learned over the course of the day. The sheriff and the doctor seemed very convinced that Harlan Edderly had died as a result of a riding accident. With a man the stature of a Harlan Edderly, O'Grady found it odd that neither man had ever even considered the possibility of murder. Then again, they were both professionals, and maybe they were just that sure. It was only the dead man's daughter, after all, who was convinced that it was otherwise.

O'Grady decided that in the morning he'd ride back out to the Edderly ranch and talk to the men who had found the body, as well as anyone else who might have seen the body. Someone might remember tracks on the ground, and what they might have meant. Again he was sorry that he couldn't have seen the scene himself. The ground could have told him a lot.

He was ordering another pot of coffee when Steve Stilwell walked in the door. O'Grady saw him and waved him over.

"Have a seat and join me," O'Grady said.

"Finished eating?" Stilwell asked, sitting.

"Just having another pot of coffee," O'Grady said. "I'll keep you company while you eat."

"Got some more questions, huh?" Stilwell asked with a grin.

"Some," O'Grady admitted.

A waiter came over and Stilwell ordered steak and potatoes.

"And bring another coffee cup," O'Grady added.

"All right," Stilwell said, when he had a cup of coffee in front of him, "ask away."

"How much do you know about Cal Festin?"

"The sheriff?" Stilwell asked. "He used to be a federal marshal before he came here."

O'Grady found that interesting. As a federal marshal, Festin would have been involved in quite a few manhunts over the years. That meant that the man should be able to read sign. If the ground around Harlan Edderly's body had a tale to tell, Festin should have been able to see it.

"What are you thinking?" Stilwell asked.

"A lot of things," O'Grady said. "The sheriff and the doctor seem damned sure that Harlan Edderly fell off his horse. They don't seem even the slightest bit willing to consider murder."

"Can you give them something that would make them consider it?"

"No," O'Grady said. "I just wish I could have seen the ground around the body."

"Meaning what?"

"Meaning if Edderly fell off his horse, then there'd be only his horse's tracks on the ground."

Stilwell nodded, but before he could say anything the waiter came with his dinner. They waited while the waiter set everything out and walked away.

"So if there were other tracks on the ground," Stilwell said, slowly, gesturing with his knife, "that would

73

support a theory that he was killed? Struck from behind?"

"It wouldn't totally support it," O'Grady said. "There could have been others with him who then left, and then he fell off, but it would at least indicate that someone could have been there with him."

"I see," Stilwell said, cutting into his steak. "Then what you need to do is talk to the first person who found Edderly."

"I understand two men found him," O'Grady said. "I'll be talking to them tomorrow."

"Good," Stilwell said. "If you find out anything I should know . . ."

"You'll be the first to know," O'Grady said. He stood up. "Enjoy your meal. When you're finished, come over to the Bull's Eye Saloon and I'll buy you a drink."

"I'll be there," Stilwell promised.

Cal Festin left his office and went looking for Willie Mayberry. Willie was the town drunk—if indeed the town had only one—and ran errands for the sheriff for drink money. The sheriff had a particular errand in mind at the moment. He finally found Willie sitting behind the livery stable. The man was muttering to himself as Festin approached him.

"Willie!"

Mayberry looked up quickly at the sound of his name, ready to run if necessary. When he saw who it was he smiled and struggled to his feet. He was in his fifties, roughly the same age as Festin, but he was frail, unwashed, and, surprisingly, sober.

"You sober, Willie?"

"Ain't nobody will give me a drink," Willie complained, "nor the price of one."

"We can take care of that, Willie."

Mayberry laughed, revealing a mouth with more

spaces than teeth, and said, "I knew I could count on you, Sheriff."

"All you got to do is run an errand for me."

"Sure, Sheriff, whatever you want."

"I want you to ride out to the Edderly place and deliver a message for me . . ."

When O'Grady entered the Bull's Eye, the evening's activities were just getting into full swing. A full compliment of girls—including Candy—were working the floor, and the poker game he had previously played in appeared to be just starting up. Taylor, the gambler, saw him enter and stood up to intercept him at the bar.

" 'Evenin', Mr. O'Grady."

"Taylor."

"Buy you a drink?"

"Sure," O'Grady said. "A beer."

"Two beers, Bill," Taylor called out, and Bill nodded.

"You going to be playing tonight?" Taylor asked.

"After awhile," O'Grady said. "Not right off, though. I'll give it a little time."

"I can understand that," Taylor said. "You've got other things to worry about besides a poker game. Unlike you, I don't. That's the way I make my living."

"I could tell by the way you played."

"You played quite well yourself," Taylor said as Bill brought the beers.

O'Grady picked up his beer and said, "I was lucky. I'm not in your league. It also helped that the other three aren't that good."

Taylor laughed.

"You couldn't convince them of that. Each of them thinks he's the best player in the world."

"I suspect those are the people you make the bulk of your living off of, Mr. Taylor."

"You've got that right, Mr. O'Grady," Taylor said.

"Good players will usually play each other to a standstill. It's the bad players we make our money off of."

"Especially the bad players who think they're good players, eh?"

In reply Taylor raised his mug and then drank half of it down. He set the other half down on the bar.

"Time to get to work. Be seeing you later."

"Sure."

Taylor took one step away, then turned and said to O'Grady, "Oh, don't underestimate your own abilities as a poker player. I'm not."

He watched Taylor walk back to the table, where the other three players all seemed anxious to begin playing. They each probably figured they were going to make back what they had lost the night before . . . and the night before that . . .

As Taylor went back to the table, O'Grady wondered what it must be like to make a living gambling. You had to be able to quickly pick out who you could beat easily and who you couldn't, who were the good players and who were the bad ones, which ones were bad and thought they were good, which ones knew they were good but pretended they were bad. It seemed to him that you probably never really knew who was who or what was what.

Come to think of it, it sounded a lot like *his* business.

11

O'Grady was still working on his beer when Candy came sauntering over.

"How are you?" she asked.

"Fine," he said. "You're looking particularly fetching tonight."

"I'll bet you say that to all the women that you've slept with for the first time on the day after."

"What?" he said, frowning.

She laughed and said, "Never mind. You going to play poker tonight?"

"I was thinking about it. Why?"

"Nothing," she said. "Just watch out for the three town fathers, that's all."

"What about them?" O'Grady said.

"Just watch 'em."

"Are you saying that they cheat?"

"I'm just saying that they play together a lot," she said, "and can generally read each other pretty good."

"But they've been losing," O'Grady said.

"I said pretty good," she added. "Not perfectly."

"Oh, I see," he said. "Well, thanks for the warning."

"I got to get back to work," she said, touching his arm. "I'll see you later?"

"I'll be waiting."

As Candy went back around the room, Steve Stilwell stepped through the batwing doors and approached the bar.

"You finished eating fast," O'Grady commented.

"I never finish my food," Stilwell said, patting his

flat stomach. "Besides, you gave me added incentive to get over here fast."

"Right," O'Grady said, "I owe you a drink. Beer?"

"Fine."

"Bill?"

"Comin' up," Bill said.

Stilwell turned and surveyed the room.

"They're at it again, huh?"

"Who?"

"The town fathers," Stilwell said. "King, Decker, and McLish."

"They play a lot together?"

"It's all they do when they're not working," Stilwell said, turning back to accept his beer. "I think they finally bit off more than they could chew."

"With Taylor, you mean?"

Stilwell nodded and sipped his beer.

"Taylor's been here a week and they've been trying to beat him all that time."

"You're not saying they've been cheating, are you?" O'Grady asked.

Stilwell stopped and looked at O'Grady for a moment.

"Did you play them?"

O'Grady nodded. "Last night."

"How did you do?"

"Real well."

"Did you notice them cheating?"

"No," O'Grady said, "but then I'm not a gambler. I don't know that I would have noticed. I'm sure Taylor would have, though."

"Maybe he did," Stilwell said.

O'Grady looked over at the four men, who were now engrossed in their game, and then back at Stilwell.

"You mean maybe he knows they're cheating, and he's beating them at their own game?"

"It's possible."

Again O'Grady thought back to the incredible run of luck he seemed to have had last night. Was Taylor dealing him cards on purpose?

"Are you going to play tonight?"

"I had intended to, yeah," O'Grady said. "To me it's just a way to pass the time."

"Well, maybe I'll pass the time watching," Stilwell said. "It might be interesting."

"Do you play?"

"I used to," Stilwell said, "but I wasn't very good. I thought I was, and I lost a lot of money before I finally admitted that I wasn't. Money, a wife, a family, and a business."

"Sounds like you learned the hard way."

"That's the way we usually learn a hard lesson, isn't it?" Stilwell asked.

The newspaperman finished his beer and said to O'Grady, "Drink up, my turn to buy."

"One more," O'Grady said. "I don't want to be drunk when I play."

"Good thinking. I used to play drunk or sober, and just as badly either way. Are you a good player?"

"To tell you the truth," O'Grady said, "at this point I'm not really sure."

After the second beer, O'Grady watched the game for the next hour with Stilwell. From what he could see, nothing had changed from the night before. Taylor still seemed to be raking in three out of every four hands.

"You see anything?" O'Grady asked.

"No," Stilwell said, "but like I said, I was a bad player. I'd be an even worse cheat. Taylor looks like he's cleaning up."

"Sure does."

"Maybe you'd be better off just sitting out," Stilwell said.

"Well, you've got my curiosity up, now," O'Grady

79

said, pushing away from the bar. "I'll just play to take a better look."

"Good luck . . ."

O'Grady walked over to the table and Taylor noticed him immediately. The second to notice him was Ed King.

"Ah, come back to give us a shot at our money, huh?" he asked.

"Just couldn't stay away from you boys," O'Grady said, sitting down.

"I wonder why?" Nick McLish said, wryly. "My deal, boys. Let's play poker. Five card stud . . ."

O'Grady played for two hours and while he wasn't as hot as he had been the night before, he wasn't losing, either. He was just about holding his own. Taylor, on the other hand, was still cleaning up. The Town Fathers—as he had come to think of the threesome—were still donating their money. It occurred to him then that it might not all be their money. As members of the town council, did they have access to money that belonged to the town? No, now he was not only thinking of them as potential cheaters, but potential thieves as well. He was probably doing them an injustice.

O'Grady decided to concentrate harder when Taylor dealt, to see if he was deliberately giving him cards.

"Seven card stud," Taylor said, and dealt out the first three.

If he was giving O'Grady cards on purpose, he wasn't being kind. The agent's first three cards were as mismatched as they could be. He decided to play for one more card, only. When it fell, however, it paired him up with a Queen he had in the hole. The other hole card—a five of clubs—and the other up card—a deuce of diamonds—were still pretty useless, but his Queens now beat anything that showed on the table.

Ed King had a pair of tens showing, and bet them timidly. Everyone else called, so O'Grady decided to sit quietly with his Queens and call as well. No one seemed to have a firm hand, and from what he could see on the table, no one was in any real danger of building one.

His fifth card was a deuce, so he now had Queens and deuces. Taylor's dealing had quickly built him something out of nothing—he had almost folded on the deal, after all. Still, he couldn't see that Taylor was doing it knowingly.

The sixth card was useless, and Ed King was still high on the table with tens, betting them warily.

O'Grady decided to raise this time.

"Ten dollars," King said.

Everyone around him called and then O'Grady said, "Raise twenty."

King sat up straight and looked at O'Grady's cards.

"What the hell do you have?" King said. He then asked the table in general, "What'd he raise on? What was the last card he got?" but nobody answered him.

Paul Decker, to O'Grady's left, said, "I fold."

"Damn it," King said, "I call." He had nothing but tens but felt he had to call because he was high on the table.

"I'll fold," Taylor said. "Mr. O'Grady looks too strong to me."

"Strong?" King said. "He's showin' nothin'!"

"You should have raised him, then, Ed," Nick McLish said, "like I am. Twenty more, Mr. O'Grady."

"What?" King said. "What do you have? You didn't raise me!"

O'Grady watched King, wondering how much of his bluster was an act. Had he and McLish set him up for this raise?

McLish had a pair of threes on the table. His other

cards were a six and a Jack. Even if he had another Jack in the hole, that only gave him Jacks over, and O'Grady's Queens over would beat that. However, if he had another three, O'Grady was in trouble.

Since they still had another card coming, O'Grady decided to call and wait to see what he got.

"I call."

"Me, too," King said, "although I don't know why."

"Last card," Taylor said, and dealt the seventh card out face down.

"Pair of tens is high," he said, and King frowned and replied, "I know it!"

They waited while King thought it over, and then said, "I check."

"Fifty dollars," Nick McLish said.

O'Grady knew then that McLish had at least three threes, and possibly a full house with either threes full or Jacks full.

"Fifty more," he said.

"Christ," Ed King said, "I'm out. Goddamned tens."

McLish studied the cards on the table in front of O'Grady. He showed nothing, absolutely nothing. A Queen, a deuce, a four, and a nine. There was not even the threat of anything on the table. All four cards were of different suits, so there couldn't even be a hidden flush.

"Call and raise a hundred," McLish said. "You're bluffing, O'Grady. You're trying to buy this hand, and it's not gonna work."

O'Grady made a show of studying his down cards again, then started picking up his money.

"Call your hundred," he said, tossing it into the pot, "and raise a hundred."

O'Grady saw Taylor nod almost imperceptibly, and suddenly felt sure that Taylor had known what he was doing when he dealt this hand. Or at least the last card.

"What the hell—" McLish said, and now O'Grady caught a glance pass between him and Ed King across the table, and he felt equally sure that they had been setting him up. Whatever they had been planning, though, Taylor had ruined for them.

"I call," McLish said, throwing his money into the pot.

"Queens full," O'Grady said. He flipped over his hole cards. Two Queens and a deuce. His full house had been totally hidden.

"Jesus," McLish said, and flipped his cards over. He had two Jacks in the hole for a full house, Jacks over threes . . . a loser. "Sonofabitch!"

O'Grady ignored him and raked in his money. He made a concerted effort not to look across the table at Taylor. He didn't want anyone watching them to think that they had been working together.

12

"Then they were cheating!" Candy said later. They had just made love and were lying side-by-side in O'Grady's bed. "They do cheat. I always suspected, but I never knew for sure."

"Well," O'Grady said, "they don't cheat, exactly."

"What do you call it then?"

"They simply work together," O'Grady said. "They catch somebody in between them who they think has a decent hand, and they build a pot. Or sometimes they'll just bet to keep him in, and then start raising each other. Meanwhile, the person between them keeps throwing his money in."

"Did that happen tonight?"

"Oh, yes."

"And what happened?"

"I got Queens full to beat Nick McLish's Jacks full."

"Wow," she said. "He must have gone crazy."

"He would have gone even crazier if he knew that Taylor made sure I got my full house."

"Taylor?" she said. "You mean . . . he purposely gave you a full house?"

"I believe so."

"Then he was cheating."

"Right," O'Grady said, "he was cheating."

"But for you?"

"I think Taylor saw what they were doing, and de-cided to step in. He simply made sure that I got that third Queen, and then sat back to see what would happen."

"So if they tried to work together to beat you, they must have been doing the same against him."

"Right," O'Grady said, "and it hasn't been working. He's been beating them, anyway."

She shook her head and said, "It sounds to me like everybody in that game is cheating, and everybody knows it, and nobody is saying anything."

"That may well be."

"Are you gonna keep playing with them?"

"I don't know," he said, frowning. "I may not have time, anyway."

There was a moment of silence and then she said from the dark, "I heard you've been asking about Harlan Edderly's death."

"I have," O'Grady said. "Do you know anything about it?"

"Only that it really had some people worried for a while."

"Worried about what?"

"About what would happen to the town."

O'Grady thought a moment and then said, "I can see that. The richest man in the county dies, and the town worries about how that's going to affect it as a whole. I guess a lot of that will depend on his daughter."

"Miss Tight Ass."

"What?" he asked, laughing.

"That's what we call her," Candy said. "She walks around like she's got somethin' stuck up her ass. Thinks she's too good to talk to the likes of us."

O'Grady assumed that "the likes of us" referred to Candy and the other saloon girls.

"Does she have any friends in town?" he asked.

"Not that I know of."

"How about her father?" he asked. "Did he have any friends in town?"

Now Candy laughed and said, "That old bull? Most of his friends were female."

"Had a lot of women, did he?"

"A few in town that he visited, and sometimes even they weren't enough for him and he'd come sniffin' around us."

"What about you?"

"I never—well, I did once," she said. "I just wanted to see what the old fella was like."

"And?"

"He had a lot of energy for a man his age," she said. Her hand snaked down his belly and she added, "Of course, not as much as you do."

Her hand massaged him until he was hard, and then she slid down and took him in her mouth. He stopped thinking about Harlan Edderly . . .

Red Atkins stood across the street from Canyon O'Grady's hotel. He was waiting for Candy to come out. If she didn't come soon, he was going to wait. He didn't want her around when he went after O'Grady. The man had made a fool out of him in front of a whole saloon full of people, and he couldn't risk that again. When he went after him this time it was going to be just the two of them. Once he had taken care of the man then he'd let everybody know.

Atkins folded his arms across his chest and fought to keep his eyes open. Another half hour and then he was gonna have to go and get some sleep and leave O'Grady for another night. The man was asking questions about Harlan Edderly, so he'd be in town for awhile, because nobody was going to be answering those questions. Nobody . . .

In the morning, O'Grady awoke alone, dressed, and went downstairs for breakfast. He decided just to have a quick one in the hotel dining room, then regretted it. The food was worse than he had remembered.

Over the last of his coffee he tried to remember the names of the women Brenda Edderly had said her father was seeing. Ivy was one, he seemed to remember. That's right, Amy Ivy and . . . Chapin? No, Chaplin, that was it. May Chaplin . . . no, Mary Chaplin.

Amy Ivy and Mary Chaplin.

He wanted to talk to them today, and to the two ranch hands who had found the body—Gorman Dwyer and Hannibal Dundee.

Since he was in town, he decided to find the women first, and talk to the hands later. He walked out to the front desk and approached the clerk.

"Can I help you, Mr. O'Grady?"

"I hope you can," he said. "Do you know a woman named Amy Ivy?"

"I sure do," he said. "Right pretty young lady she is, too."

"Where would I find her?"

"She works in the dress shop, down the street a couple of blocks, on the other side."

"I see. What about Mary Chaplin?"

"Mary? I know Mary. She runs a rooming house at the south end of town. Uh, you're not thinking of staying somewhere else, are you? Is there something wrong with your room?"

"No," O'Grady said, "there's something wrong with the food, but not with the room. Thanks for the information."

"Sure," the man said, "anything I can do to help."

O'Grady left the hotel, turned left, and walked until he saw the dress shop across the street. As he watched, a woman opened the door and walked in, so he knew it was open. He crossed the street and looked in the window. The woman was the only customer, and behind the counter was a pretty woman just a few years older than Brenda Edderly. He assumed that this was Amy Ivy. He also assumed that she would not want to talk about her relationship with Harlan Edderly in front of a customer, so he waited until she was finished serving the woman. When the lady left he quickly went inside before another customer could come along.

The woman behind the counter was obviously surprised to see a man in the shop.

"Can I help you?" she asked.

She was shorter and slighter than Brenda, but was extremely pretty, with an impish smile that she was showing now.

"Uh, yes, I hope so."

"What size are you?" Amy Ivy asked, and then laughed behind her hand.

"That's very funny," he said. "Are you Amy Ivy?"

"Yes," she asked, still stifling her laughter.

"I'd like to talk to you about Harlan Edderly."

That stopped her laughter cold, and she dropped her hands to her sides.

"What about Harlan?" she asked.

"His daughter has asked me to look into his death."

"Why would Brenda do that?"

"She doesn't think her father died by accident," he said.

"That's silly," Amy Ivy said. "Everybody knows he fell off his horse."

"How does everybody know that, Miss Ivy?"

"Well . . . I don't know, they just know."

"I understand you had a close relationship with Harlan Edderly, Miss Ivy."

She stiffened and said, "Who told you that?"

"Brenda."

"Harlan and I were . . . friendly."

"I'm really not interested in what you did behind closed doors, Miss Ivy. I'm more interested in anything he might have said to you, oh, maybe the week before he died."

"Like what?"

"I don't know," O'Grady said. "I'd like you to tell me that."

"I don't understand—"

"Did he say anything about being in danger?" O'Grady asked. "Maybe something about someone threatening him? Anything like that?"

"No . . . no, nothing like that."

"Are you sure?"

She frowned, searching her memory.

"I'm sorry, Mister . . ."

"O'Grady," he said. "Canyon O'Grady. Listen, Miss Ivy, I'm staying at the hotel down the street. If you can think of anything he might have said, would you let me know? Please?"

"Of course," she said. "Of course I will, but I don't think—"

"You'd like to know if someone killed him, wouldn't you, Ma'am?" he asked.

"Well, of course I would," she said.

"All right, then," he said. "That's all I'm asking of you, is to help me find out if someone killed him."

"I'll—I'll think about it."

"Good," O'Grady said. "That's all I ask. Thank you very much."

"Yes . . . all right," she said, still unsettled and unsure.

"Can you tell me how to get to the rooming house?" he asked.

"The rooming house? Yes, just keep walking south until you reach the end of town. You can't miss it."

"Thank you."

He headed for the door and she asked, "Are you going to see Mary Chaplin?"

"Yes, I am."

He waited to see if she was going to say anything else, and when she didn't, he left.

13

O'Grady found the rooming house with no problem and knocked on the door. From inside came the wondrous smells of baking, and his mouth started to water. The door was answered by a handsome woman in her mid-forties. She had gray-streaked brown hair worn behind her head, and clear brown eyes. Her skin was clear, as well, although beginning to show the signs of age. There were lines where once there were none, but couldn't that be said for everyone? Her figure had probably once been trim, but there was now a matronly quality to the hips and breasts. Still, she was very attractive.

"Can I help you?" she asked. "Are you looking for a room?"

"No, Ma'am," he said. "I'm looking for Mary Chaplin."

"Well, I'm Mary Chaplin," she said. "But if you're not looking for a room I don't know what I can do to help you."

"My name is Canyon O'Grady, Miss Chaplin."

"It's 'Mrs.,' " she said, correcting him. "I'm a widow."

"I'm sorry," he said, "Mrs. Chaplin."

"What can I do for you, Mr. O'Grady?"

"I'm helping Brenda Edderly find out what really happened to her father," he said.

She looked mildly surprised and said, "I thought everyone knew what happened to Harlan."

"No," he said, "everyone thinks they know what happened to him."

"And you know?" she asked.

"Brenda thinks he was too good a horseman to just fall off his horse, Mrs. Chaplin."

She took a moment before saying, "Well, that's true enough. Harlan was wonderful on a horse—but that doesn't mean he didn't fall off."

"No, Ma'am, it doesn't," O'Grady said. "It just gives me cause to ask some questions."

"Like what?"

"Like who had reason to kill Harlan Edderly?"

She stepped out onto the porch and let the door close behind her, then folded her arms across her chest and regarded O'Grady critically.

"If you've already talked to other people, Mr. O'Grady—Brenda included—you already know that Harlan was a hard businessman. He was tough and he was successful. That combination makes for a lot of enemies."

"There are enemies, Mrs. Chaplin, and then there are enemies," O'Grady said. "I'd bet there are a lot of people who wished Harlan Edderly dead, but how many of them would have taken steps to make that wish come true? Very few, I think. Those are the ones I'm looking for."

"I can't help you with that, Mr. O'Grady," Mary Chaplin said. "I didn't know anything about Harlan's business. It seems to me Brenda could help you more with that, or Jarrod Burke."

"Jarrod Burke?"

"Harlan's attorney."

"Does he have an office here in town?"

"Here, and in San Francisco," she said. "Harlan was Jarrod's biggest client, but he has others."

"Is he in town now?"

"I think he is. He came back when he heard about

Harlan's death. He's trying to help Brenda manage Harlan's business affairs other than the ranch."

"Where would I find his office?"

"He has an office in the courthouse building," she said. "That's the new brick building right in the center of town."

O'Grady remembered seeing the building as he walked around town.

"I appreciate you speaking to me, Mrs. Chaplin," he said.

"Mr. O'Grady," she said, "I don't know that I accept that Harlan didn't die by accident, but if he didn't, I stand ready to do what I can to help you."

"I appreciate that, Mrs. Chaplin," he said, "and I'm sure Brenda will, too."

"Brenda and I don't get along too well, Mr. O'Grady," she said, "but you tell her what I said, anyway. I'm here to help her in any way I can."

"I'll tell her, Ma'am."

"And don't call me 'Ma'am,' " she said. "My name is Mary."

He extended his hand and said, "My name is Canyon."

She took his hand and shook it firmly.

"From what I can smell, you're a very fine baker, Mary," O'Grady said.

"I get by," she said, releasing his hand. "Come back around supper time and I'll let you sample some."

"I just may do that, Mary," he said. "Thanks."

He stepped down off the porch and headed back to the center of town. Mary Chaplin watched him until he was out of sight, then turned and went back inside. She wanted to bake a very special pie, now.

O'Grady walked to the courthouse building and stood across the street. On the second floor he saw a large window with *Jarrod Burke, Attorney-at-Law* written on it in big block letters. Underneath in smaller letters it said *Little Bend, Wyoming & San Francisco, California.*

He crossed the street and entered the building. Inside he found a stairway to the second floor and ascended. There were several doors on the second floor, but one had the same writing on it as the window. He approached it, knocked, and entered. He found himself in a small outer-office. There was a desk, but no one was seated at it. There was the smell of perfume in the air, though, so he assumed that Burke had a secretary or clerk who simply was not there at the moment.

There was a door behind the desk that said PRIVATE on it. He walked to it and knocked. He heard the sound of footsteps behind the door, and then it opened abruptly.

"Jenny, I thought I told you—Oh!" The man took up sharply when he saw O'Grady.

"I'm not Jenny," O'Grady said.

"Of course you're not," the man said. He stuck his head out the door and looked around. "Where did that girl get to?"

"She wasn't here when I arrived."

"She's looking to get fired," the man said. He straightened and stared at O'Grady.

"I take it you're Jarrod Burke," O'Grady said.

"That's right. Can I help you?"

"My name is Canyon O'Grady, Mr. Burke," O'Grady said, "and I'd like to talk to you about Harlan Edderly."

"He's dead," Burke said without hesitation.

"I know," O'Grady said. "That's what I want to talk to you about."

Burke looked around again for some reason, then stepped back and said, "Come in."

O'Grady entered, and Burke closed the door and walked around his desk.

O'Grady was a little surprised that Burke was so young. He didn't look forty yet. The agent thought that a businessman like Harlan Edderly would have had a longtime attorney, and so was expecting someone of a comparable age. Burke was tall, well-built, with wavy brown hair and a carefully tended mustache.

"Have a seat, please," Burke said, seating himself behind his desk. "Are you some sort of law enforcement agent?"

"No," O'Grady said easily, "just someone who wants to help Brenda Edderly."

At the mention of the girl's name, a small smile came to Burke's lips.

"There are quite a few of us who would like to help Brenda, if she would let us." It was obvious that Burke had some feeling for Brenda. O'Grady wondered also about the foreman, Pete Gentry. Brenda Edderly was certainly attractive enough to attract male admirers under normal circumstances. Now, however, she was also a wealthy young lady.

"Is this about Harlan not dying accidentally?" Burke asked.

"Brenda's already spoken to you about that, huh?"

"She's spoken to anyone who will listen," Burke said. "I guess she finally found someone who was willing to do more than listen, eh? Or are you being paid to do more?"

"No money is changing hands, Mr. Burke."

Burke narrowed his eyes and said, "I am naturally suspicious of situations where help is being offered without some sort of payment, Mr. O'Grady."

"I guess there's not much I can say to that, Mr. Burke," O'Grady said. "What do you think of Brenda's suspicions?"

"They're hardly suspicions, Mr. O'Grady, are they?" Burke asked.

"What are they, then?"

"The ramblings of a daughter who has lost her father tragically, and refuses to accept it."

"Brenda Edderly did not strike me as the kind of girl who rambles, Mr. Burke," O'Grady said.

"Certainly you don't put any credence in her . . . her claims."

"It's kind of hard for a superb horseman to just fall off a horse, Mr. Burke."

"It's been known to happen."

"You accept it, then?"

Burke spread his hands in a helpless gesture and said, "What else can I do?"

"Well, you might have hired a detective to look into it when it happened," O'Grady said. "I'm working a cold trail here."

"Too cold, I'd say."

"All the more reason why it should have been investigated back then."

"It was."

"By the town sheriff?" O'Grady asked. "That's hardly an investigation, Mr. Burke."

"The doctor—"

"The doctor said that Harlan Edderly died from a blow to the head," O'Grady said. "I'm questioning how that blow was received."

Burke folded his hands and touched the tips of both index fingers to his lips.

"Mr. O'Grady," he said, finally, "I really don't think there's any point in pursuing this. Harlan's dead, I'm helping Brenda with his business holdings, Pete Gentry is helping her with the ranch. There's really nothing for you to help her with that I can see."

O'Grady stood up, not so much because it sounded like a dismissal but because he wanted to leave. He was getting nowhere with Jarrod Burke.

"We have a difference of opinion there, Mr. Burke," the redheaded agent said. "One that I don't think we're going to resolve here and now. Good-day."

Burke opened his mouth to reply, but closed it abruptly and watched O'Grady leave his office. He stood then to stare out his window, watching for O'Grady down on the street. He looked across the street then and saw Sheriff Festin standing outside his office, also watching O'Grady. Suddenly, Festin looked up and his eyes met those of the attorney. Burke set his right index finger alongside his nose for a moment, then moved away from the window.

Cal Festin waited until Canyon O'Grady had walked far enough away before he walked down the street to the doctor's office. There were no patients with Green when he entered.

"Marty, we've got a meeting tonight," Festin said.

"With who?" Green asked, nervously.

"With everybody," Festin said. "Gentry, you, me, and Burke."

"And the others?"

"We'll talk to the others after we talk to each other," Festin said. "Just be there, Burke's office."

"What time?"

"Same time as always, damn it," Festin said. "Don't go dumb on me, Marty."

"All right, all right," Green said, testily. "I'll be there."

Instead of leaving then, Cal Festin put his hand roughly on Green's arm and squeezed. Marty Green winced at the pain, but did not try to pull away.

"We got to do what we got to do, Marty," Festin said. "Remember that."

"Yeah," Marty Green said, "yeah, I'll remember that, Cal. There isn't much chance of me forgetting it."

Festin released his arm and said, "See that you don't," before walking out.

O'Grady walked away from the courthouse and pretended that he didn't see the sheriff watching him from across the street. He also noticed the sheriff look up at the window of Jarrod Burke's office. There was more going on here than met the eye, and probably more people involved than Festin and Burke.

His intention now was to ride out to the Edderly place to talk to the two hands who originally found the body. While he was there, though, he'd have another talk with Brenda Edderly, and maybe even with Pete Gentry as well.

O'Grady suddenly had the feeling that all he had to do was keep on pushing, and somebody would eventually push back.

14

As luck would have it, Pete Gentry saw O'Grady riding up to the house and moved to intercept him. O'Grady did not dismount to talk to the man, who was barring his path.

"What do you want?" Gentry demanded.

"Well, for one thing I want to talk to you," O'Grady said. "But first I want to talk to the two hands who found Harlan Edderly's body."

"I don't remember who they were."

"Let me refresh your memory," O'Grady said. "Gorman Dwyer and Hannibal Dundee."

Gentry's jaw tightened.

"I tell you what," O'Grady said, and this time he did dismount. "You round those boys up for me while I talk with Miss Edderly. When I come out of the house, I'll be ready for them."

He started for the house and Gentry put his hand on the agent's chest. "Don't think I'm gonna let you get away with this, O'Grady," the man said.

"Get away with what, Gentry?"

"Taking advantage of Brenda."

O'Grady smiled and said, "I think the lady is too smart to let anyone take advantage of her, Gentry. Not me, and not you."

"Pete!" Gentry didn't turn, but O'Grady saw Brenda Edderly standing on the porch. "Let him pass!"

O'Grady watched Gentry's face run a gamut of emotions before the man finally lowered his hand.

"And take care of my horse," O'Grady said, handing the man his reins. O'Grady walked toward the porch then, and could feel Gentry's stare burning into his back.

"Come inside, Mr. O'Grady," Brenda said. "I'll get some coffee."

"Sounds fine," O'Grady said. He followed the woman into the house without looking back at Gentry.

Inside, Brenda led him to a den rather than the office. "My father did as much business in this room as he did in his office," she said, indicating the book-lined walls. "I'll get that coffee."

She left O'Grady alone in the room. He was tempted to prowl the room, examining the shelves, but instead sat in one of the overstuffed armchairs that dominated the center of the room. She returned shortly with a tray; on it was a pot of coffee and two cups. She set the tray down on a table between the two chairs and sat across from him. She then poured the coffee and handed him a cup.

"What was that all about?" she asked.

"You mean your foreman? I think he thinks he's protecting you from me. Like everyone else, he probably thinks I'm charging you a lot of money to look into your father's death."

"Who's everybody?"

"Well, Jarrod Burke, for one."

"Oh," she said, and her face was as unreadable as her tone.

"Had he been your father's attorney for long?" O'Grady asked.

"No," she said, "Jarrod's father was my father's attorney for years. When he died, Jarrod took over the firm and father just stayed with him."

"I got the impression that he has . . . strong feelings toward you."

"Jarrod thinks he's in love with me," she said.

"And Gentry?"

She looked at him and said, "You don't miss much, do you? Yes, Pete, too."

"Is there anyone else you know of who's in love with you?"

She looked at him sternly and said, "You're making fun of me."

"No," he said, "I'm not. I really want to know."

She frowned, then said, "No, there's no one else that I know of."

"How did they each feel about your father?" he asked.

"They both had employee/employer relationships with my father. Jarrod's father was the only man I knew of who ever worked for my father who was also his friend. Do you think that one of them—Jarrod or Pete—had something to do with my father's death?"

"I don't have enough information yet to make an assumption like that, Brenda."

"What have you found out so far?"

"Not much," he said. He told her all of the people he had talked to, and that he had come to the ranch now to talk to the two hands who had found her father's body.

"Is that what you and Pete were talking about?"

"Yes," he said. "He tried to tell me he didn't recall their names."

She frowned again and said, "I'll have to talk to Pete. He's going to have to be more cooperative with you."

"Why don't we just leave it the way it is?" he asked, putting his cup down. "If you tell him to be more cooperative, it's more than likely he'll become even less cooperative—if that's possible."

"That's childish."

"I know," he said, "but I think that's the way it will go."

"All right," she said. "You'll have to handle Pete yourself, then."

"I intend to," he said, standing. "He should be getting those two men for me right now."

"Come and see me before you leave, all right?" she asked, also standing.

"I will," he said. "Thanks for the coffee. I'll see myself out."

He left the den, found his way to the front door, and left. Once on the porch he saw two men standing at the foot of the steps. They turned as he started down the steps.

"Dwyer? Dundee?"

"That's right," one of them said.

"Which is which?"

The spokesman said, "I'm Dundee, he's Dwyer."

Dundee was the bigger man, heavy through the torso, with a thick black beard. Dwyer was smaller, sandy-haired, with a nose that looked as if it had been smashed flat more than once.

"The boss said we was supposed to talk to you," Dundee said. "About what?"

"Harlan Edderly."

Dwyer frowned and said, "He's dead."

"I know," O'Grady said. "I want you two to ride with me out to where you found him. I want to ask you some questions."

"I don't know," Dundee said. "We got work to do. All the boss said we was to do was talk to you."

"I tell you what," O'Grady said. "Why don't we ask Miss Edderly what you should do, hm?"

The two men exchanged a look, then Dundee said, "We'll saddle our animals."

"Get mine, too," O'Grady said. "I think Gentry put him in the stable."

Dundee nodded and the two men walked off to the big stable. They returned minutes later with their own horses and Cormac.

"Let's mount up," O'Grady said, accepting his reins

from Dundee. "I don't want to keep you men from your work for too long."

They rode out to the place where the two men had found Harlan Edderly's body, and dismounted.

"Why were you fellas riding this way?" O'Grady asked.

"We was just riding back to the ranch."

"And you saw him?"

"Gorman saw him," Dundee said. "He said he saw what looked like Mr. Edderly's horse."

"Where was the animal?"

"Off that way a few yards," Dundee said, "just grazing."

"So you came over to check it out."

"That's right."

"And found what?"

"We found Mr. Edderly laying on the ground."

"Show me."

"Huh?"

"Show me where he was laying."

Dundee walked over to the big rock Edderly had supposedly struck his head on and said, "He was lying right here."

"No," O'Grady said, "I mean show me. Lie down on the ground the way he was lying."

"Huh?"

"Go ahead."

Dundee looked over at Dwyer, who frowned and shrugged. The bigger man then got down on the ground and stretched out on his stomach near the rock.

"Like that?" O'Grady asked. "He was lying just like that?"

"Well . . . yeah," Dundee said. He craned his neck to look at Dwyer and said, "Wasn't he lying just like this, Gorman?"

"Sure was," Gorman said. "Just like that."

"And there was blood on the rock?"

"Yeah, there was," Dundee said. "Can I get up now?"

"Sure," O'Grady said, "sure, you can get up."

Dundee got up and brushed himself off.

"See?" he said. "He fell off his horse and hit his head on the rock."

"I see," O'Grady said, but that wasn't what he saw. What he saw clearly for the first time was that Harlan Edderly had been murdered.

"Were there any other tracks on the ground?" O'Grady asked.

"Whataya mean?" Dundee asked.

"Just what I said," O'Grady said. "Tracks on the ground. Edderly's horse must have left some tracks."

"Of course it did."

"Well, what about other tracks? Maybe left by other horses?"

"There might have been some," Dundee said. "I don't rightly recollect. You, Gorman?"

"No," Dwyer said, shrugging, "I don't recall."

"Can we go back to work now?" Dundee asked.

"Sure," O'Grady said, "sure, and I'll ride back with you."

"Did you find out anything?" Dundee asked as he mounted up.

"Something," O'Grady said, "I found out something."

He found out that a man who was supposed to have fallen off his horse and struck the back of his head on a rock, cracking it open and killing himself, had been found lying on his stomach!

To Canyon O'Grady it sure looked like Harlan Edderly had been murdered.

O'Grady decided not to tell Brenda what conclusion he had come to about her father's death. In fact, he didn't want anyone to know what he had decided, not

104

until he could figure out some way to prove it and find out who had actually done it.

Actually, once he did figure out a way to prove it, he was going to have to try to find out who he could prove it to. He didn't trust the law in Little Bend at all.

He stopped just long enough to tell Brenda that he'd be in touch. As he rode out he was aware of Pete Gentry standing off to the side, staring hard at him. He didn't worry about that. He wanted to get back to town and send some telegrams.

15

"Red."

Red Atkins stopped and turned around to see who was calling him. He was surprised when he saw that it was Sheriff Festin calling from an alley he had just passed.

"Sheriff?"

"Come 'ere, Red," Festin said. "I want to talk to you for a minute."

Red looked around, then walked over to where Festin was. The sheriff backed into the alley, and Red followed.

"What is it, Sheriff?" Red asked. "I ain't done nothin', you know."

"I know, Red, I know," Festin said. "That's what I wanted to ask you about. Do you have any plans to get even with that Canyon O'Grady character?"

"Sheriff," Red said, "I can't tell you that. You might—"

"Look, Red," Festin said, "this is just between you and me, right? Just two men. Forget about the badge. You do want revenge, don't you?"

"Well, sure . . ."

"I mean, especially since he's going around telling everybody how easy he whipped you."

Red frowned and said, "What? He is?"

"Sure he is," Festin said, "and I don't like it, Red. You know why?"

"No. Why?"

"Because you live in this town, Red," Festin said,

slapping Red on the shoulder. "I mean, you're one of us and he's a stranger. You know what I mean?"

"Sure, I do . . . I think."

"Red," Festin said, "I want you to know that I'll back you. You just do what you got to do, and I'll be behind you all the way."

"I appreciate that, Sheriff," Red Atkins said, still puzzled.

"And I'll tell you something else," Festin said. "There are others in town who feel exactly the same way."

"There are?"

"And I mean some big people," Festin said. "People who would pay you plenty if O'Grady didn't walk away next time. You know what I mean, Red?"

"Yeah, I think so," Red said, then frowned and said, "Uh, you ain't tellin' me I got to kill him, are you, Sheriff?"

"Would I tell you that, Red?" Festin asked. "I'm just saying you do what you got to do, and if you happen to fix O'Grady real good, well, there's some extra money in it for you—like this."

Festin took out fifty dollars and handed it to Red Atkins, whose eyes widened when he saw how much it was.

"Holy—Sheriff, that's fifty dollars!"

"And it's yours, Red," Festin said. "And there's more where that come from. Don't let O'Grady get away with the grabbing, Red. It makes you look bad, and it makes the town look bad. Do you understand me, Red?"

"Sure, Sheriff," Atkins said, "sure I do. I understand you real good."

"Good, Red," Festin said, slapping the other man on the back, "real good. Now, remember, this little talk was just between you and me, huh?"

"Sure, Sheriff," Red said, lowering his voice, "just between you and me."

"Okay," Festin said, "put your money away and go on about your business, okay?"

"Sure, Sheriff." Red pocketed the money and left the alley, looking for Canyon O'Grady.

When O'Grady rode back into town, he had already composed the telegram in his mind. In a hostile town—and he had come to think of Little Bend that way—he had to be careful when he sent telegrams to Washington, especially since this one was going to be asking for some help. He needed some federal law in town so that he'd have someone he could trust watching his back, someone who would have the authority to act when he came up with the evidence he needed.

He rode directly to the telegraph office, dismounted, and secured Cormac before going inside.

"Help ya?" the clerk asked.

"I'd like to send a telegram."

"Sure thing," the man said. He took a pencil from behind his ear and said, "Go ahead."

"I think I'd better write it down myself."

"Sure," the clerk said. He pushed the paper and pencil across the counter and stood there watching. O'Grady thought about asking for some privacy, but what was the difference? The man would see it soon enough.

O'Grady wrote his telegram, checked it over and then pushed it across the counter to the clerk.

"Expectin' a reply?" the man asked.

"Not immediately," O'Grady said, although he wasn't expecting a reply at all. Hopefully his reply would come in person. "If one comes, I'll be at the Overland House."

"Overland House," the man said, "sure thing."

"I'll wait while you send it," O'Grady said.

The man stared at him a moment, then said, "Okay, sure. I'll send it right now." The man looked at it for the first time and said, "Washington, D.C., huh?"

"That's right," O'Grady said, "Washington, D.C."

The man read the rest of the message to himself, while moving his lips soundlessly.

UNCLE CANYON NEEDS A DOCTOR.

"That's it?" the man asked, looking at O'Grady. "I mean, we got a doctor in town, you know."

"I know," O'Grady said. "Send it."

"Sure, Mister, sure," the man said. "I'm sending it."

O'Grady waited until the message was sent, then paid for it and left, taking Cormac back to the livery stable.

"I couldn't help it, Sheriff," the clerk said to Festin later on in the sheriff's office. "He made me send it while he was standing there."

"That's all right, Claude," Festin said. "You go on back to work now."

"Did I do the right thing by comin' to you, Sheriff?" the man asked, anxiously.

"You did the right thing, Claude," Festin said. "I won't forget. Now go on back to work."

As Claude left, Festin looked down at the message on his desk and read it: UNCLE CANYON NEEDS A DOCTOR.

He didn't know what the message meant, but he knew one thing. Pretty soon Canyon O'Grady was going to need a doctor.

When Red Atkins saw Canyon O'Grady crossing the street, he knew this was his chance. Not only would he get his revenge, but he'd make some extra money for himself while doing it.

He stayed across the street and kept pace with O'Grady until he was sure that the man was going to the Overland House. Once he knew that, he broke off and hurried to the back of the hotel . . .

* * *

Canyon O'Grady saw Red Atkins and wondered if he was going to have to deal with the man today. The last thing he needed now was to get into it with him again. As he approached his hotel, however, he lost sight of Atkins. He was satisfied that the man hadn't approached him, or entered the hotel after him. Maybe the man had decided not to start something today. Whatever his reason for giving up, O'Grady was glad of it.

In the lobby, O'Grady stopped short and thought a moment. What should his next move be? He'd satisfied himself that Harlan Edderly had been murdered, but how was he supposed to find out who did it? Everybody was so intent on the accidental death theory that the real murderer could have been anyone in town. The sheriff, the doctor, the lawyer, the foreman, they all seemed to want Harlan Edderly's death to stay an accident.

But who was the one who had really nailed it down as an accident? That had to be the doctor, and if O'Grady could get Doc Green on his side . . .

Instead of going up to his room as he had intended, O'Grady once again left the hotel and headed for the doctor's office.

Red Atkins entered the hotel through the back door, made his way to the second floor, and stood at the end of the hall, waiting for Canyon O'Grady to enter his room. Once the man was inside, he'd be trapped, and Red Atkins could go on about his business.

He stood at the end of the hall watching the steps thinking, anytime now . . .

16

When O'Grady entered the doctor's office, the outer room was empty and the door to the inner room was closed. He listened at the door and heard a low drone of voices. He assumed that the doctor was with a patient, and sat down to wait. Before long the door opened and the doctor came out with another man.

"Just don't use that arm for a while, Carl, and it should be fine," Green was saying.

"Thanks, Doc."

"Sure—" Green said, and stopped short when he saw O'Grady sitting there.

"Well . . . I'll be seein' you, Doc," the patient said, and when Green didn't answer the man just walked out.

"What do you want?" Doc Green asked nervously.

"Just to talk, Doc," O'Grady said, standing up. "I said I'd want to talk to you again, didn't I?"

Green's eyes darted about the room, and then he moved to the window and looked outside.

"You look worried, Doc," O'Grady said. "Worried that somebody saw me come in? A lot of people saw me come in. Anybody in particular you might have had in mind?"

"No," Green said, moving away from the window, "of course not. Look, I have patients—"

"You're not too busy now, though. I tell you what. As soon as one comes in I'll leave," O'Grady said. "How's that?"

"Look," Green said, "there's nothing more I can tell you—"

"Sure there is, Doc," O'Grady said. "You can tell me why everybody is so all fired anxious to have Harlan Edderly's death be an accident."

"It was an accident!"

"No," O'Grady said, "not the way it was set up. I mean, if it was an accident, it didn't happen the way it was set up, the way you and everybody else says it happened. If it was an accident, then tell me now how it really happened and I'll go away—if I believe you, that is—because you see, I think the man was murdered."

"Nonsense."

"And I think you know who killed him."

"That's crazy!"

O'Grady decided not to say anything more, especially not about the position of the body. In fact, he thought that maybe someone else ought to know what he knew, in case something happened to him.

"All right, Doc," O'Grady said, "I just wanted you to know that I was willing to listen. If you get the urge to talk, come and find me, okay?"

"There's nothing to talk—" Green started to protest, but O'Grady was already out the door before he could finish his sentence.

Anxiously, Green slammed the door closed and stood with his back to it.

Outside, O'Grady looked across the street and saw Sheriff Festin watching him. He touched his hand to his hat and walked away from Doc Green's door.

Festin, Green, and who else knew what had happened, and were anxiously trying to keep it a secret? Did Gentry know? And Jarrod Burke? Who else in town knew? Did the whole town know, or was that paranoid thinking?

As he had decided in the doctor's office, O'Grady

knew he had to talk to someone, but who? Certainly not Brenda Edderly. If something happened to him and she cried wolf—again—no one would believe her. He needed someone with good standing in the community, someone whose word would be respected. He thought of two people. One was Mary Chaplin, except that she had been emotionally involved with the dead man.

That left Steve Stilwell, the newspaper editor.

"That's quite a story," Stilwell said.

They were in his office, sharing swigs from a bottle of whiskey. O'Grady had just told him what he'd found out about the position of the body, and what he thought it meant.

"What do you think?" O'Grady asked.

"Let me get this straight," Stilwell said. "The body was lying on its stomach, even though he was supposed to have fallen off his horse backward and struck the back of his head on the rock?"

"That's right."

"Couldn't he have been conscious for awhile, and turned himself over?"

"Doc Green himself said that Edderly would have died instantly from the blow."

"Yes, but the doctor also said that Edderly died by accident, and you don't believe that. Why should you believe anything he says?"

For a moment O'Grady felt his resolve being shaken, and Stilwell saw that.

"Okay, listen," Stilwell said, "I believe you. I agree with you. I think Harlan Edderly was killed, too."

"But you made a good point—"

"Never mind," Stilwell said, wringing one hand up and down to set aside O'Grady's complaint. "Men like Harlan Edderly don't die by accident, Mr. O'Grady—"

"Canyon."

115

"They just don't, Canyon," the man went on. "That's one of Steve Stilwell's facts of life."

Stilwell passed O'Grady the bottle and the agent took a quick pull from it.

"What do you intend to do now?" Stilwell asked.

"I don't know," O'Grady said. He decided not to tell the newspaperman that he had sent for help. After all, he didn't know for sure that he could trust the man. Maybe, he thought, maybe he should share this with Mary Chaplin, as well.

"Well, I'm glad you told me," Stilwell said. "I mean, just in case anything happens to you."

"Yeah, but maybe I've put your life in danger now," O'Grady said.

"I don't think so," Stilwell said. "I've written a lot of crap about this town in my paper, about Edderly, and about the town fathers, and no one's killed me yet. I'm not worried about that."

"What do you think, Steve?" O'Grady asked. "Green is definitely nervous about something, Festin's concerned, even Edderly's own lawyer seems convinced that he died by accident. Could they all be hiding something?"

"If one of them killed Edderly," Stilwell said, "why would the others hide it?"

"I don't know," O'Grady said, starting to get an idea. "Maybe I should be trying to find out what Harlan Edderly's death means to everyone."

"What do you mean?"

"I mean," O'Grady said, warming to his subject, "who gains anything from having his death declared an accident?"

"His daughter?"

"She inherits no matter what," O'Grady said. "No, it's not Brenda."

"Then who?"

"I don't know," O'Grady said, standing up. "But maybe that's what I should try to find out next."

"Canyon, I'd be real careful if I was you," Stilwell said. "You're a stranger in a strange town, without anybody to back you up."

"I know that," O'Grady said. "Thanks for your concern, Steve."

"I just don't want to be writing your obituary," Stilwell said. "At least not until I get the real story about all of this."

"And maybe not even after that," O'Grady said, "huh?"

He went to Mary Chaplin's rooming house next.

"I expected you for pie after dinner," she said when she answered the door.

"Dinner?" he said.

"Haven't you had dinner?" she asked.

"Uh . . . no, I guess I forgot about it."

"You poor man," she said, taking his arm. "Come inside and I'll fix you something while we talk."

She fixed him a feast made of leftover meat loaf and vegetables, and while he ate he explained his thinking to her.

"I'm not really surprised by this," she said when he was finished. "And yet . . . I feel stunned. I mean, to think that someone from this town murdered Harlan. His ranch keeps this town going. Why would someone kill him?"

"Maybe it wasn't someone from the town," O'Grady said. "Maybe it was a business enemy, like we talked about earlier."

"Poor Harlan," she said, shaking her head. "Do you think it was wise to confide in Mr. Stilwell?"

He shrugged and said, "As wise as it is to confide in you, I guess. I know both of you equally well—which is to say not at all."

"I see what you mean."

"Then again," he said, smiling and pushing his

empty plate away, "all he gave me was a few friendly sips of his whiskey."

"And I have peach pie, as well."

"And coffee?"

"Of course."

When he had the pie and coffee in front of him he said, "I guess I'll have to hope that at least one of you is trustworthy."

"And which of us would get your vote?" she asked.

"You, I guess."

"And why is that?"

"Well," he said, "you know about him, but he doesn't know about you."

"I see," she said. "If I'm not trustworthy, then you've put him in danger."

"I hope I haven't done that."

"Don't worry," she said, "you haven't. I haven't killed a man yet."

"Mary, do you know any of the men involved? Doc Green? The sheriff? Jarrod Burke?"

"I know them all," she said. "When Sheriff Festin first came here, he stayed with me. Of course, that was a lot of years ago. I go to Doc Green when I'm not feeling well, but then so does everyone. He's the only doctor in town."

"That means that Harlan Edderly saw him, too?"

"That's right."

"What about Burke?"

"Well, I only know Burke from what Harlan told me about him, and to say hello to him on the street."

"And what did Harlan say about him?"

"That Jarrod thought that he was twice the man his father was, while he wasn't even half the man."

"If he felt that way, why did he continue to do business with him?"

"Out of respect for his father, I suppose."

"If Burke thought that Harlan was going to take his business away from him, do you think he'd kill him?"

"I don't think I can comment on that, Canyon," she said. "I don't know Burke well enough."

"I know," he said, "it wasn't a fair question."

He thought a moment about who else might be involved, and then asked, "Do you know Pete Gentry?"

"I know of him," she said. "Harlan thought highly of him. He even hoped that Pete and Brenda would get married someday."

"Really? I know that Gentry's in love with Brenda, but I didn't sense that the feeling was returned."

"It's not, that I know of. Uh, Jarrod Burke is also in love with her."

"I figured that out."

"I can understand it, I guess," she said. "She is young and pretty."

"There's a lot to be said for mature women, Mary."

"Well," she said, "thank you, sir."

He sat back and said, "I can't thank you enough for this meal."

"It was my pleasure," she said. "I love sitting and watching a man eat heartily."

"Did I do that?"

"You did," she said, laughing, "and I enjoyed every minute of it."

"Not as much as I did, I can assure you," he said, standing up.

She walked him to the front door and said, "Canyon, thank you for confiding in me."

"Well," he said, "you did say that you wanted to help."

"Well, I hope I won't have to," she said.

"Why's that?"

"If I have to tell someone everything you've just told me," she reminded him, "it will mean that you're dead."

He scratched his cheek and said, "Good point."

17

O'Grady went looking for Nick McLish, who owned the livery, the feed & grain, and the gunshop, and who was one of the town fathers.

"Hello, Nick," he said, finding the man behind the counter of the gunshop.

"Hey, poker buddy," Nick said, smiling expansively. "Gonna give us a chance to get our money back? I was just headin' over there, myself."

"Maybe we could talk a little first, Nick," O'Grady said.

"Sure, about what?"

"Harlan Edderly."

The smile faded and McLish said, "What do you want to know about that bastard?"

"You didn't like him?"

McLish snorted and said, "I did business with the man. Nobody who did business with him liked him, O'Grady. Then again, you didn't know him, did you?"

"I'm trying to get to know him."

"What are you talking about?" McLish asked. "He's dead."

"And you're not sorry, are you?"

"Hell, no . . . wait a minute," McLish said, catching himself before he could say more. "I heard somebody was asking questions around town about his accident. Is that you?"

"It's me."

"You don't think it was an accident, do you?" McLish asked, his tone accusing.

"No, Nick, I don't."

"And you think I did it?" McLish said. "Hey, I didn't like the sonofabitch, but I didn't kill him!"

"I didn't say you did, Nick," O'Grady said. "I just said I wanted to talk about him."

"Oh," McLish said, "oh . . . okay. Whataya want to talk about?"

"You and the other members of the town council," O'Grady said. "Ed King, Paul Decker . . . how many others?"

"Four," McLish said. "Sam Kenton, who owns the bank; Asa Dent, he owns the hotel; Doc Green; and Jarrod Burke."

"Burke? I thought he split his time between here and San Francisco."

"He took his old man's seat on the council," McLish said. "What do you want to know, O'Grady? We got a poker game waitin' for us."

"Edderly's death can't be a good thing for Little Bend, Nick," O'Grady said. "No matter how much you disliked him. Isn't that right?"

"It sure is," McLish said. "If his daughter can't make a go of his ranch, and his businesses, this place could turn into a ghost town. Hey, that's another reason why I wouldn't have killed him. I'd be takin' a chance of killin' my own home, my own business. That makes sense, don't it?"

"Yep," O'Grady said, "it sure does."

"Can I go to the game now?"

"Sure, go ahead."

They left the store together and McLish locked up.

"What about you? You comin'?"

"Maybe later."

"You got our money and we want it back, O'Grady," McLish said. "Give us a shot."

O'Grady nodded and said, "Probably later."

"See ya then."

As Nick McLish walked away, O'Grady thought

that what Nick had said went for all of the other members of the town council—hell, for all of the merchants in Little Bend. Killing Harlan Edderly would be like killing the goose that laid golden eggs. That meant that almost no one in town had a reason to kill him, and that everyone had a reason to want him alive.

So why wasn't he?

Red Atkins finally realized—after only about fifteen minutes—that Canyon O'Grady was not coming up to his room. Feeling foolish—and having further reason to stomp Canyon O'Grady—he left the hotel and took a position across the street. He'd wait there all night if he had to, until O'Grady did come back to his hotel.

O'Grady wanted to go to the saloon, if only to see Candy, but he didn't feel like playing poker. He decided to go back to his hotel.

"Is everybody here?" Jarrod Burke asked.

"Everybody who's coming," Cal Festin said. He looked around at Doc Green and Pete Gentry. "I thought the four of us ought to talk before we brought the others in."

"What are we gonna talk about?" Gentry asked.

"O'Grady," Festin said.

"He's pushing, Cal," Marty Green said. "He's pushing hard!"

Gentry sneered and said, "And he's pushin' the right one, too, ain't he, Doc? What'd you tell him?"

"I didn't tell him anything," Green insisted.

"Sure," Gentry said, "you're dying to bust wide open, ain't you?"

"That isn't true—"

"That's enough," Jarrod Burke said. He didn't shout, but his tone was firm enough to bring about silence.

"We're going to have to decide what to do about O'Grady, Jarrod," Pete Gentry said.

Burke gave Gentry a withering look. He hated it when the foreman called him by his first name. He also hated Gentry because he knew that the other man had slept with Brenda—at least once—and he had not.

"I've taken care of that," Festin said. "At least, I hope I have."

"What do you mean?" Burke asked. "What did you do, Cal?"

"I had a talk with Red Atkins."

"O'Grady had a run-in with Atkins, right?" Burke asked.

"That's right," Festin said.

"What'd you say to Atkins?"

"Only that O'Grady had been braggin' around town what he did to him, and that it might be worth money to him to make sure that his revenge really hurts."

Burke thought that over and then asked, "Can Atkins handle that?"

"I doubt it," Gentry said.

"I think he can," Festin said firmly, looking over at Gentry.

"Atkins is a brute with no brains," Gentry said. "O'Grady will eat his lunch."

Burke stared at Gentry, who he thought was a brute with no brains. However, Gentry knew men, and Burke was inclined to listen to him.

"Maybe we should get Atkins some help," he said.

"It's too late for that," Festin said. "I think Atkins is going to go after him tonight."

"You told Red to kill O'Grady?" Green asked.

"I told him it would be nice if O'Grady couldn't walk around and brag for a while."

"Once Red gets started, he'll get carried away," Green said. "He will kill O'Grady."

"He might," Festin said.

"He won't," Gentry said.

124

"We'll see," Burke said. "We'll just have to wait and see."

O'Grady entered the hotel and went directly up to his room this time. He'd just about decided to skip the poker game tonight. He had a hunch Candy would come looking for him anyway, once she was finished with work. Or maybe she wouldn't. That'd be fine, too. He was beat from all the running around he'd done that day. He also wasn't thinking exclusively about Candy, of late. He'd started thinking about other women, like Brenda Edderly and Mary Chaplin.

He entered his room, removed his shirt, then his gunbelt, hanging it on the bedpost. He was crossing the room to the pitcher and basin when his door suddenly slammed open.

Red Atkins, who had kicked the door open, jumped into the room with his gun in his hand.

O'Grady never paused. He kept moving, grabbed the basin of water and turned, hurling the contents of the basin at Red Atkins. Atkins instinctively raised his hands up over his head as the water drenched him.

O'Grady continued to move. He leaped across the bed, grabbing for his gunbelt. As he tumbled to the floor he yanked the belt free of the bedpost and grabbed for the gun itself.

Atkins had succeeded in only partially shielding his head from the water. Some of it hit him in the face, and he was frantically wiping it from his eyes with one hand now, while fanning the room with the other, his gunhand. O'Grady fired, out of instinct. There was no conscious thought behind it at all.

The first bullet struck Atkins in the side, spinning him around and slamming him against the wall. Atkins's finger jerked on the trigger, firing once into the ceiling, and then O'Grady fired again as Atkins was bouncing off the wall. The big man ran right into the bullet. It punched through his throat with a sickly, wet sound and went out the back of his neck. A huge red mushroom appeared on the wall behind him and he fell to the floor like a rag doll.

O'Grady got to his feet, moved to the body, then bent and pried the gun from Atkins's dead fingers. People began to congregate in the hall, trying to get a look inside the room.

"Somebody get the sheriff," he said. They continued to stare into the room and he said in a harsher tone, "Will somebody go and get the sheriff . . . now!" and then closed the door in their faces.

He sat down on the bed and stared down at the dead man. This did not seem to him the way Atkins would have gone after his vengeance. The man struck O'Grady as the type who would rather have gotten his revenge with his bare hands. What had possessed the man to come after him with a gun?

Or who?

He stood up, put his shirt back on, retrieved his holster and donned it. This had all the earmarks of a setup. He had a feeling things were going to get ugly now, and he wanted to be fully dressed and prepared.

18

O'Grady could tell from the commotion outside that the sheriff had arrived. When Festin entered O'Grady's room, he had a man in tow whom O'Grady had never seen. The man was wearing a deputy's badge. He had no way of knowing if the man was a regular deputy, or if he was just along for this particular incident.

"Sheriff," O'Grady said.

Festin ignored him and leaned over Red Atkins to examine him.

"He's dead, all right," O'Grady said. "Although you might want to get Doc Green over here to give you an opinion on how he died."

"I don't need you being smart with me, O'Grady," Festin said. "This is serious."

"Of course it is," O'Grady said. "I always take killing a man serious."

"Well, maybe not as serious as I do," Festin said. "I don't take kindly to murder in my town."

"Murder?" O'Grady said. "What the hell are you talking about?"

"Everybody saw that you and Red had a run-in your first day in town. He probably came up here to clear things up, and you killed him."

"Oh sure, Festin," O'Grady said, "and I kicked my own door open, too."

Festin turned and looked at the door. The lock had been splintered by Red Atkins's kick.

"That door could've been like that when you checked in for all I know."

"Now listen, Festin," O'Grady said, "I'm not just going to let you railroad me into a murder charge."

"You don't have much choice, O'Grady," Festin said. "We'll let a judge decide whether you are or aren't a murderer. Give me your—"

Before Festin could finish, O'Grady drew his gun and backed off a step.

"Sorry, Sheriff," he said, "but you're not leaving me much choice in the matter. Stand easy, Deputy. Toss your gun on the bed. Do it now!"

"Do it," Festin said.

The deputy removed his gun from his holster and tossed it on the bed.

"Now the sheriff's."

Festin moved his arm away from his body so the deputy could get to the gun. The man tossed it on the bed next to his own.

O'Grady moved to the window, opened it, then collected the guns from the bed and threw them out the window.

"You're not making this easy now, O'Grady," Festin said.

"Nothing's going to be easy, Sheriff," O'Grady said. "I'm going to prove that Harlan Edderly was murdered, and that you, and Doc Green, and probably Jarrod Burke were all in on it."

"That's crazy."

"Maybe," O'Grady said, "but when I get the proof I need, it'll be you facing a judge, not me."

There was a low roof just outside the window and O'Grady decided that he'd leave that way.

"If either of you poke your head out of this hotel before I'm gone I'll shoot it off," he told them. "Understand?"

"Sure, Mister," the deputy said, but Festin just kept staring at him.

"We'll be seeing each other again, Sheriff," O'Grady promised.

"You can count on it, O'Grady."

O'Grady pushed the window open as wide as it would go and stepped out onto the roof, still covering the two men. He knew that once he was out the window the men would move, so he was going to have to move fast.

He ran to the edge of the roof and saw that the drop to the alley below was not that steep. He holstered his gun, shinned over the side, hung down by his hands, and then dropped. He felt a jarring impact in his ankles and knees, but no damage was done.

He ran to the back of the alley, not wanting to run down the town's main street.

What he needed now was a place to hide.

"Let's move!" Festin said as soon as O'Grady went out the window.

"But Sheriff," the deputy said, "he said—"

"Never mind what he said," Festin said, opening the door, "follow me!"

The crowd in the hall parted to let the sheriff through, then closed up again to try and see in the room again. The deputy had to push his way through to follow the sheriff.

O'Grady ran along behind the hotel, and when he came to a high fence he scrambled over it. Dropping down on the other side, he caught his left hand on a nail, tearing open the palm.

"Shit!"

It was dark, which was in his favor. He could hear voices coming from the hotel and knew that Festin and the deputy had come out the front door. The first thing they'd do was retrieve their guns, so he still had some time to put distance between himself and the hotel.

He knew now that Festin had sent Red Atkins after him. If Atkins killed him, then he was out of everyone's hair, and when he killed Atkins, it gave Festin the chance to lock him up—if he could catch him.

However, this also worked in Festin's favor. How could O'Grady move about, gathering his evidence, when he was on the run? Well, he was going to have to find a way to do it, otherwise he'd be on the run for a long time.

His mind was working frantically as he ran, trying to come up with a hiding place. He felt sure that Brenda Edderly would hide him; after all, he'd gotten into this situation by trying to find out what happened to her father.

Hiding at the Edderly ranch was out, though, at least for tonight. Maybe in the morning he could get himself a horse and ride out there. What he needed was a place to hide tonight—and he could only think of one.

In the alley, Festin and his deputy picked their guns up from the ground.

"Keep going up this alley," Festin told the man. "Keep looking for him."

"Alone?" the deputy asked.

"I'll get more men!" Festin snapped. "Now go, before he gets away."

"Y-yessir."

As the deputy went deeper into the alley, Festin went back to the front of the hotel.

"I need some men to help in the search for Canyon O'Grady," he said loudly as the people from the hotel surged into the street. People on the street, hearing the commotion and seeing that something was going on, also crowded around to find out whatever they could.

"Come on, come on," Festin called out, "I need a

damned posse. Let's have some volunteers or I'll start picking people out."

And in the end that's what he ended up doing . . .

O'Grady made his way to the south end of town and around to the back of Mary Chaplin's house. He chanced a look in the window and saw her in the kitchen. He went to the back and knocked on the door, not loudly, but insistently, until she answered.

"Canyon—" she said, but he quickly quieted her.

"Let me in," he said, and slid past her. "Close the door."

She did so, frowning.

"What's wrong?"

"I killed a man tonight," he said. "The sheriff's after me."

"And you came here?"

"You don't understand," he said. "The sheriff sent the man to kill me, and I killed him first. Now he says he wants me for murder. He's probably putting a search party together right now."

"I see," she said. "I never did like the way Cal Festin did his job."

"He's good at it," O'Grady said, "which is what worries me."

"Don't worry," Mary said, "they won't find you here."

"How many boarders do you have in the house now?" he asked.

"Four," she said, "but their rooms are upstairs. Mine's down here."

"Yours?"

She nodded.

"That's where you'll be staying. Even if the sheriff comes here with his search party, he wouldn't dare look in my room."

"I hope you're right."

"I know I am," she said. "Come on, I'll show you where it is, and then—is your hand bleeding?"

He looked down at his left hand, which was indeed bleeding, and badly.

"Sorry," he said, "I got it on your floor—"

"Don't worry about that," she said. "I can clean it. Come on, we'll go to my room and I'll clean and bandage that. I'm sure you could use a drink, too."

"Maybe just one," he said.

She put him in her room and then returned with a basin of water, some clean cloth, and some bandages. She cleaned the wound, which was ragged, and bound it tightly.

"How did you do that?" she asked.

"On a nail, I think."

"Hopefully it won't get infected. Don't use that hand," she said. "That wound needs to be stitched, and if you try to use it you'll start it bleeding again."

"You do that very well," he said.

"I've had practice," she said. "Wait here, I'll get you something to drink."

He expected her to come back with some sort of brandy or sherry, but when she returned she was carrying a half-full bottle of whiskey.

"I didn't bring a glass," she said, handing it to him.

"That's all right," he said. He accepted the bottle and took a deep pull from it.

"That's enough," she said, taking it back. "I don't need you to be drunk."

"I need to clean up," he said. His clothes were dirty, and other than the hand she had just cleaned, he was covered with dirt from the alleys he had been hiding in.

"I'll bring more water and some soap," she said. "I think I might have a clean shirt somewhere, too."

"I appreciate the trouble you're going to, Mary," he said.

"Never mind," she said. "I've never yet turned a soul in trouble away from my door."

Waiting for her to return with the water and the shirt, he suddenly felt very tired, but the one thing he couldn't afford to do now was fall asleep. He had to stay awake and alert. Festin would be searching the whole town for him tonight, and he doubted that the man would stop. This was his chance to discredit O'Grady completely, so that whatever he had to say about Harlan Edderly's death would fall on deaf ears.

Mary brought the water, soap, and shirt in and watched him while he washed awkwardly with one hand. Afterward she helped him on with the shirt.

"Does this all have to do with Harlan's death?" she asked.

"Yes," he said. "I'm convinced that Festin and a lot of other people in this town know what really happened or are behind what really happened, and they don't want the truth to get out."

"Do you know the truth yet?"

"No," he said, "but I'm going to find out, and the only way I can do that is to stay free."

"Well then," she said, "I suppose we'll have to do what we can to make sure you stay that way, won't we?"

that then he had "volunteered" reached the south
in Texas. O'Grady could hear their tension so that
her Mary came in to tell him he already knew.

19

It was a good couple of hours before Festin and some of the men he had "volunteered" reached the south end of town. O'Grady could hear them outside so that when Mary came in to tell him he already knew.

"They haven't come to my door yet," she said, "but my boarders are curious now. Just make sure you don't leave this room."

"Maybe this wasn't such a good idea for you, Mary—" he started, but she cut him off.

"It's too late for that kind of thinking now," she said. "Just stay hidden!"

He nodded and she left the room and closed the door behind her.

O'Grady's injured hand—his left, luckily not his gunhand—was feeling stiff and painful, and he remembered what she said about hoping it wouldn't get infected. He had seen men lose limbs to infection, but he couldn't start thinking about that now. He had enough to worry about without adding that.

He figured to leave Mary's house before first light and try to get himself a horse—that is, if he couldn't get Cormac from the livery. After that, he'd ride out to the Edderly ranch. With any luck they wouldn't have heard about the shooting yet, and they wouldn't be on the lookout for him . . .

He heard the pounding on the front door and came alert. He stood up, palmed his gun and moved to the door of the room. He cracked it open just enough to hear what was going on.

"Can I help you, Sheriff?" he heard Mary Chaplin ask.

He couldn't hear everything Festin had to say, but he could fill in the blanks.

"We're looking for a killer, Mrs. Chaplin."

"In my house?"

"Well, maybe he got into your house without you knowing it."

"Sheriff, you know me long enough to know that no one gets into my house without me knowing it. I can assure you there are no killers in my house."

"Well . . . I'll leave a man nearby, just in case he shows up."

"Fine," Mary said. "I feel safer already."

He heard her close the door, and then she came down the hall toward him. He backed away as she opened the door and stepped inside.

"I heard," he said. "He gave up pretty easy."

"Cal Festin knows he can't push me around," she said. "He's leaving a man near the house, though. You may not be able to slip out."

"I'll wait until morning, just before first light, and then try it," he said.

"That means you'll have to sleep here."

"I don't have to sleep."

"Of course you do," she said. "How are you going to be able to keep alert if you don't get some sleep? I can sleep on the sofa in the living room."

"If one of your boarders sees you out there, they'll become suspicious."

"Well then, we'll just have to share the room," she said. "We can do that for one night, can't we?"

"Sure we can," he said.

"Sure we can," she said.

While the search was still going on, Festin went to Jarrod Burke's office to see him. Burke often worked in his office until late into the night.

"So it didn't go as planned, eh?" Burke asked as the lawman entered his office.

"O'Grady killed Red," Festin said, sitting across from the lawyer, "but that can still work in our favor."

"How?"

"O'Grady is on the run now," Festin said. "He escaped from me when I tried to arrest him. Who's gonna listen to an escaped murderer?"

"I still don't like it," Burke said. "We'd be better off if he was dead."

"That can still be arranged."

"Sure," Burke said, "all you have to do is find him."

"I'll find him."

"You better send someone out to the Edderly ranch to tell Gentry what's going on," Burke said. "Since O'Grady is working for Brenda, he might try to go out there."

"Right," Festin said, "I'll take care of it."

"That's what you should have done as soon as this man got to town, Festin," Burke said. "You should have taken care of it."

"I take care of everything, Burke," Festin said. "Just remember that."

"Get the others together for a meeting tomorrow, downstairs," Burke said. "It's time everybody got in on this."

As Festin left Burke's office, he thought about his retirement. Although it was not far off, maybe it was time to move the timetable up a bit. When this was all over, he'd turn in his star and take that retirement while he still could.

Doc Green sat in his office, his hands clasped together on his desk next to a bottle of whiskey that was more empty than full. This whole thing had gotten out of hand.

He poured a drink and downed it. How had he let

himself get involved in this? Was he afraid? Was he greedy? Or was he just incredibly stupid?

That must have been it, he decided. He was incredibly stupid to let Festin, Burke, and Gentry get him to agree to do what he did.

And now Canyon O'Grady could bring the whole town down around their ears—which was the very thing they had all been trying to avoid in the first place.

There had to be a way out, he thought. There had to be some way for him to get out from under without going to jail, and without getting killed. If he went to O'Grady, the others would kill him. If he waited for O'Grady to come looking for him, he would probably go to jail. Of course, he could just wait for the others to kill O'Grady—but what if the man didn't kill easily? What then?

He poured himself another drink . . .

Out at the Edderly ranch, Pete Gentry was watching the house. From where he stood, leaning against the wall of the stable, he could see Brenda Edderly's room. The light was lit, and he could see her shadow moving about inside. He took a pull from the whiskey bottle he was holding and told himself he was a fool for not going up there. For not marching right up to the damned house, letting himself in, going up to her room, and just taking her, there and then. He didn't want her that way, though. He wanted her to want him. He wanted her to come looking for him, to realize that he was the man for her, the only man she could ever count on.

Jesus, he thought, sucking on the bottle again, if she ever found out . . . if she ever knew what part he'd had in her father's death, that would never happen . . .

He couldn't let Canyon O'Grady find out, and then tell her. He'd kill the man before he let that happen.

He turned when he heard the approaching horse. Maybe this was a message from town. Maybe Festin had taken care of O'Grady once and for all.

"All right," Mary said, reentering the room. She was now wearing a robe, and underneath it a nightgown. She smelled fresh and clean.

O'Grady had simply removed his shirt and boots. His intention was to sleep in his pants. He didn't want Mary getting nervous about having agreed to share the room—and the bed—with him.

"Which side of the bed do you want, Canyon?" she asked him.

"Oh, I don't know," he said, "which side do you usually sleep on?"

"I'm usually alone, Canyon," she said. "I sleep on the entire bed."

"Oh, yeah, right . . ."

"When I was married," she said, "I slept on the right side. Why don't we do it that way?"

"Sure," he said, "I'll sleep on the left side. No problem."

"Fine." She started to remove her robe, then stopped abruptly and asked, "This isn't going to make you nervous, is it?"

"What? Oh, you mean taking off your robe? No, of course not."

"Because if it is I'll keep it on."

"No," he said, "Mary, you don't understand. I'm usually not nervous around women. I thought you'd be nervous about this."

"Me?" she asked, dropping the robe on a chair next to the bed. "Why would I be nervous about this? It's not as if I was a virgin. After all, I was married once, and I've . . . had men in bed with me before."

"Of course you have."

"Why would you think I'd be nervous?"

"I don't know," he said. "I just thought—you know, a strange man—"

"A *younger* man?" she said, arching an eyebrow at him. "Was that what you were thinking? I'd be nervous because you're younger?"

"No, of course not," he said. "Being younger or older has nothing to do with it."

"Tell me something, Canyon," she said. "You've had a lot of women, haven't you?"

"A lot? Well, what's a lot—" he said, thrown off balance by the question.

"Many women?"

"Well, yes, I've had, uh, many women—"

"Younger as well as older?"

"Some younger, some older, yeah," he said, wondering what she was leading up to.

"And do you think all the women you meet want to go to bed with you?"

"No," he said, "of course not . . . not all the women I meet—"

"But a fair amount, right?"

"Well—"

"I mean, you're big, you're attractive, and women like you, right?"

"Well . . . most of the time."

"And do you know how to treat a woman?"

"I like to think so," he said, "yes."

"So then why are we beating around the bush with this?" she asked.

Suddenly, she unbuttoned her nightgown and removed it, dropping it on top of the robe on the chair.

"Um," he said, transfixed.

She had heavy, well-rounded breasts, wide hips, long legs with good, solid thighs. He was willing to bet that she had never been a small woman, not even as a young girl. Her nipples were wide and brown, and were tightening as he watched.

"Didn't you expect this?" she asked.

"Well, no," he said, "to tell you the truth, I didn't."

"Well, good," she said, getting on the bed on her knees and reaching for him. "I would have hated it if I was being predictable."

She hooked her fingers in the front of his trousers and pulled him to her. They kissed, tentatively at first, and then more deeply, mouths opened, tongues probing . . .

Breathlessly she asked, "Are you going to keep these pants on all night?"

20

"Harlan never laid a hand on me," Mary said.

"What?"

"He never touched me," she said, and then laid her hand on his belly and said, "at least not this way."

"But I thought—"

"Yes, I know," she said. "That's what his daughter thought, too. It's what everyone thought."

"And you didn't mind?"

"No," she said, "I didn't mind. Harlan was my friend. He came here to talk, to spend some time away from . . . from everything."

"It seems to me if he was such a good friend he wouldn't have wanted everyone to think that something was going on when it wasn't."

"Oh, he wanted to tell people," she said. "I wouldn't let him."

"Why?"

She turned her head and looked at him and said, "Because he was my friend."

They made love a second time. The first time was frenzied, which surprised him—until she told him that she and Harlan had never had sex. She also told him that it had been a long time for her, and then he understood.

The second time, though, was slow and sweet. He kissed her breasts, holding first one and then the other in his hands, cradling them, making love to each of them. He suckled her nipples until she cried out for him to stop—and not to stop.

He lowered himself onto her then, pressing the head of his penis against her moist portal, teasing her, letting his rigid length rub over her, letting the larger head of his penis prod the smaller head of her clit, and then she reached for him, closing her hands over his buttocks, and he let her pull him into her, but slowly, an inch at a time until he was nestled firmly inside of her. She lifted her heavy thighs then, wrapped her powerful legs around him and he began to move, ever so slowly, withdrawing from her and then sliding back in, all the way in, so slowly that it was almost painful . . . for both of them.

She arched her back, thrusting her breasts up to him, and he leaned over and kissed them. As his lips touched her nipples she spasmed and began to buck beneath him. He quickened his tempo then and exploded inside of her so that they both experienced their pleasure peak at the same time.

"I'm curious," he said, later.

"Ask."

"What about the other woman? What's her name?"

"Amy," she said, "Amy Ivy. You know, I think Harlan was sleeping with her."

"Really?"

"That surprises you?"

"Well, she was significantly younger than he was," O'Grady said.

Mary smiled and said, "Good for Harlan."

He turned his head and looked at her, saw her smiling.

"Didn't that bother you?"

"You mean, was I jealous?"

"I guess that's what I mean."

"No," she said. "We were friends, Harlan and I. If he was happy, I was happy. He came here to talk and

144

eat. He apparently went to Amy to . . . take care of other needs. That was fine with me." They were silent a moment and then she asked, "Does that make sense to you?"

"Yes, I guess it does," he said.

"Haven't you ever had a woman for a friend? I mean, a real friend?"

"You mean without sex being involved?"

"That's right."

He thought a moment and then said, "I don't think so."

"I think that's sad," she said. "Now I'm sorry that we had tonight."

He frowned and said, "Why?"

"Because I would have liked to teach you how to have a woman friend."

He put his hand on her belly, then slid it up over her ribcage until he was cupping one of her breasts. She caught her breath as his thumb touched her nipple. She had extremely sensitive nipples.

"I'm not sorry," he said, leaning over and kissing the space between her breasts.

She sighed, cupped his head in her hands, and said, "No, I guess I'm not, either."

In the morning—while it was still dark—they got up and dressed. They had both gotten very little sleep, but neither of them was complaining.

"How's your hand?" she asked.

"It's all right."

She knew he was lying. Once during the night, while they were making love, he was on top and put too much weight on the hand. He cried out, but later said that it hadn't hurt that much.

"You're a liar," she said then, and now she said the same thing.

He looked at her, then smiled and said, "You're right. It hurts like hell."

"Let's take a look at it," she said.

He sat on the bed and she unwrapped his hand. The wound was red and raw, and the hand was bruised, but she saw no indication that there was any infection.

"It's bruised," she said, "but clean of infection. That's good."

She removed the old bandage completely, and the wound began to seep.

"This really needs to be sewn," she said.

"So sew it," he said.

"What?"

"Do it."

"With what? I don't have the proper equipment."

"You have needle and thread, don't you?"

"Well, of course—"

"Then use it," he said.

"Canyon, I can't—"

"Can you sew?"

"Of course I can."

"Then sew it," he said. "I've got a lot to do, Mary, and anything you can do to make sure this hand doesn't hinder me will help. If it starts bleeding I won't be able to stop to take care of it."

"Oh . . . damn," she said, after a moment. "All right. I'll get the needle and thread."

She came back with the needle, thread, and a candle. She lit the candle, then held the needle in the flame. She threaded the needle then, complaining that it was hot, and he extended his hand to her. She took hold of his wrist and settled his hand into her lap.

"This is going to hurt like hell," she said.

"I know," he said. "Do it."

With one hand she held the edges of the wound together, and with the other she inserted the needle, pulled the thread through, and then repeated the process until the wound was closed.

"I didn't make the stitches too close together," she said. "I didn't want there to be so many of them."

She leaned over and used her teeth to break the thread, then tied it off.

O'Grady hadn't said a word the entire time. He couldn't, because he had his teeth clenched tightly together so that he wouldn't yell.

"All right," she said, "let me bandage it again."

She put a clean bandage on it, this one not as tight since the stitches would keep the wound closed.

He flexed the hand slowly and said, "You should have been a doctor, Mary."

"I've done enough of it over the years to qualify," she said.

"How many years?"

"Canyon!" she said, slapping his uninjured wrist. "None of your business."

She offered to make coffee, but he declined it.

"On second thought," he said, then, "make it and bring it to the sheriff's man outside."

"Why should I bring him coffee?" she demanded.

"Because," he said, "while you're bringing it to him, and talking to him, I'll slip out of the house and try to get to my horse."

"That's silly," she said. "The livery stable is bound to be covered. I've got a horse out back in a small lean-to. Take that one."

"Is he a saddle horse?"

"He could be," she said. "I use him for my buggy, but I've got an old saddle back there you could use."

He thought it over. There was no sense trekking to the other end of town if he didn't have to take the chance. And he didn't need a fast horse to get to the Edderly ranch, just a horse.

"All right," he said. "Make that coffee and take it to the man."

She went to the kitchen and the aroma of coffee

quickly filled the house. O'Grady hoped that none of her boarders would wake early and be enticed downstairs by it.

She came back into the room and said, "I'm ready."

"You'll have to locate him first," O'Grady said. "My guess is he's out front."

She left and returned moments later.

"I looked out the front window. There's a man across the way."

"All right, take him the coffee and talk to him."

"What do I say?"

"I don't know. Sympathize with him that he had to be out there all night. Say anything, just make sure you give me about ten minutes."

"Ten minutes," she said. "All right, I'll try." She kissed him quickly and said, "Be careful."

"I'm always careful."

"Tell that to your hand," she said, and left.

He moved through the darkened house as she went out the front door. He peeked out the front window and saw her approaching the man, who straightened quickly.

Cal Festin awoke and frowned. For a moment he didn't know where he was, then realized that he had gone to sleep in a bunk in one of the cells. He'd only meant to take a nap, but had obviously fallen asleep for longer than that.

The search last night had not turned up much—hell, it hadn't turned up anything. This morning he was going to check with the man he'd left at the Chaplin house. If anything had happened during the night—which was doubtful, since no one had woken him—then he'd ride out to the ranch. That'd be the logical place for O'Grady to try to get to.

Actually, it might even be better to catch him out there. They could kill him without having to explain anything to anyone in town.

He stood up, rubbed both hands over his face vigorously to try to wake himself up, then donned his hat and left the office.

O'Grady quickly moved through the house, to the kitchen, and out the back door. In the lean-to, he found the old saddle Mary Chaplin had talked about. It was well-worn and cracked, but still usable—and much the same could be said for the horse.

As he tried to saddle the animal, he wished he had asked for more than ten minutes. His injured hand was making it a difficult task, but he finally got it on and cinched tightly. His bandaged hand was screaming in protest, and he was thankful for the stitches Mary had provided him with. She had gone well beyond the call of duty in helping him. He only hoped he could think of a good enough way of thanking her.

He walked the animal out of the shack and away from the house, walking straight back, keeping the house between him and the sheriff's man. At the same time he held his hand over the horse's muzzle, trying to keep the animal quiet. When he judged that he was far enough away from the house not to be heard he mounted up. The horse, not accustomed to wearing a saddle or a man, tensed, but O'Grady spoke to it gently until he could feel the animal's muscles relax beneath him. That was all he needed, to be thrown by some old buggy horse.

"All right, boy," O'Grady said, patting the animal's neck, "let's see if we can get to the Edderly ranch without you, me or the saddle falling apart."

21

Getting to the ranch without falling apart was not going to be as hard as getting there alive.

When O'Grady reached the spot where Harlan Edderly's body had been found, he reined the buggy horse in and dismounted.

"This is where you get off, boy," he said, tying the horse's reins to the tree. "I've got to go on foot the rest of the way."

He realized now that getting to the ranch in the dark would have been easier. But the sun wasn't quite up yet, and there was no heat to deal with. He figured he could cover the few miles between there and the house before it got too hot, and before he was spotted. Sure, there'd be early morning activity around the ranch, but he doubted the hands would get mounted up and out into the countryside before he could reach the house. Even if they did, there was ample cover for him to duck behind. A man afoot actually wasn't all that easy to spot, not if he was wary—and Canyon O'Grady had every intention of being that.

"She did what?" Festin asked his man.

"She came out and gave me some coffee, Sheriff," the man said. "It really hit the spot, too."

"You fool," Festin said. "Why would she do that? Did you ask yourself that?"

The man shrugged and said, "I just figured she was being nice, is all."

"Sure, nice," Festin said. "She liked the way you looked, right?"

"Aw, Sheriff," the man said, "I'm too homely for that."

"You sure are," Festin said, "and you're stupid, too."

Festin turned to walk away and the man called out, "You want I should still watch the house?"

Festin didn't answer. He walked around to the rear of the house, where he knew Mary Chaplin kept a horse—only the horse was gone.

"Damn!" he swore.

O'Grady had to be on his way to the Edderly ranch. He had a head start, but he was riding an old buggy horse. He wouldn't be too hard to catch up to.

The sheriff thought about going into the house and lighting into Mary Chaplin for helping the man, but that could wait until later. Instead, he stalked away from the house, intending to saddle his own horse and head for the Edderly ranch himself.

Mary Chaplin was watching through the front window when Sheriff Festin joined his man outside. She watched them speak, and Festin seemed angry. When the sheriff walked away she ran to the back door and looked out as Festin checked on her horse. For a moment she thought the lawman was going to come to the house, but instead he walked away. He had obviously figured out what had happened and now he was going to chase Canyon O'Grady.

Mary sat at the kitchen table, her hands clasped nervously in front of her, and wondered what she could do to help now.

O'Grady remembered from his previous visits to the Edderly house that there was a rise just behind it. He figured to approach the house from that direction.

He'd be out of sight unless someone was watching when he topped that rise.

When he reached it, he dropped to his belly and crawled to the top. He could see the back of the house, and a little beyond it. From what he could see there was plenty of early morning activity. Before he could safely approach the house, he was going to have to wait for the hands to mount up and begin to go about their jobs. Once the bulk of them had ridden away he'd try descending the rise to the rear of the house.

He settled in to wait.

In her father's office, sitting at her father's desk— she still thought of these things as her father's— Brenda Edderly wondered how long she could go on with this. Maybe she should just forget about finding out what really happened to her father. Maybe she should just sell the damn ranch and get the hell away from Little Bend and Wyoming. Even before selling the ranch, she certainly had enough money to go anywhere she wanted to go. How would O'Grady feel, she wondered, if she tried to call him off now? And did she want to?

She sat back in her father's chair and folded her arms across her chest. No, by God, she didn't want to. Sure, she'd sell the ranch and move away, but not until after she proved that her father had been killed.

And not until the guilty party was brought to justice—or, if it could be arranged, until she killed them herself!

O'Grady waited well over an hour before he finally decided to move. There were undoubtedly still some hands in front of the house, in the corral, working around the stables, but he thought he could get to the rear of the house without them seeing him—providing none of them decided to come around to the back of the house.

He got to his feet and started down the rise. He was running in a crouch and laughing at himself. As if running in a crouch would keep him from being seen, right?

Finally, he reached the back wall of the house and realized that he had been holding his breath. He took a moment to let his breathing return to normal and then started looking for a way into the house. As it turned out, the back door wasn't even locked. He had seen a woman come out the back and had assumed that she was a cook. Obviously, she had not bothered to lock it behind her—lucky for him.

He entered the house and found himself in a hallway. Ahead of him he could see the kitchen, so he moved to his left, moving slowly and quietly. He passed a doorway and saw the dining room. If he remembered correctly from the times he had been in the house he would be moving in the direction of the office.

Finally, he reached the end of the hall and saw that he had indeed come to the office. He moved to the door and peered inside. Seated behind the desk was Brenda Edderly, and she was alone.

"Brenda," he said, stepping into the room.

He frightened her and she started, half rising.

"You startled me."

"I'm sorry."

"How did you get in?"

Before answering he closed the office door behind him.

"I came in the back way," he said. He moved past the desk to the window to look outside.

"What's wrong?"

He looked at her and said, "I had to kill a man yesterday, and now the sheriff is after me."

"Did it have something to do with my father?"

"Sort of." He explained the incident with Red Atkins, and how the sheriff apparently had used it to send Atkins after him.

"Why would the sheriff do that?" she asked.

"Because I think he knows what really happened to your father," O'Grady said. "In fact, I think a lot of people know what happened to him."

"Do you know what happened to him?" she asked.

"Not exactly," he said, "but I am pretty sure he didn't die by accident." He explained about the position of the body and how it led him to the conclusion that her father had been struck from behind and killed, and then placed on the ground near the rock to make it look like an accident.

"I knew it!" she said, slapping her palm down on the desk. "How do we prove it?"

"Well," he said, "that's going to be a little hard with the sheriff out looking for me."

She was about to say something when they both heard a horse approaching. They moved together to the window to look outside.

"It's the sheriff," she said.

"He figured I'd come out here."

"He's alone," she said.

"That doesn't mean anything," he said. "He can get all the help he needs from out here."

"My men?" she said.

"Gentry's men," he said. He explained that the men who worked on a ranch usually looked at the foreman as the man—or person—they worked for. "They'd be loyal to him."

"And you think that Pete was in on what happened to my father?"

"He's the foreman, Brenda," he said. "They'd almost have to include him."

"And who else?"

155

"The doctor, Jarrod Burke, the other men on the town council."

"You make it sound like the whole town killed my father," she said.

"I hadn't thought about it in those terms," he said, rubbing his jaw, "but maybe they did."

22

"What are you talking about?" she asked. "How could a whole town kill someone?"

"Not the whole town, exactly," he said. "Just the people who run the town. Tell me something; was your father thinking about selling the ranch?"

"How did you know that?"

"I didn't," he said. "I just guessed."

"What would that have to do with his death?"

"Think about it," he said. "If your father sold the ranch and left Wyoming, what would that do to the town?"

"Nothing," she said. "Whoever bought the ranch would keep it going."

"Maybe," he said, "and maybe the town fathers didn't want to take a chance."

"So they killed him to keep him from selling?"

He shrugged.

"What about me?" she asked. "I'm thinking about selling. Are they gonna kill me?"

"Maybe they didn't think it through that far," he said. "Maybe they just figured that if they killed your father, the ranch would go on the way it had been, with Pete Gentry running it."

"This is crazy," she said, shaking her head and putting her hands to her temples.

O'Grady looked out the window again and saw Sheriff Festin talking to Pete Gentry.

"I saw a lot of the men ride out this morning," he

said to her. "How many would be left on the grounds?"

"Maybe half a dozen, depending on what Pete had them doing."

"That's too many."

"Wait here," she said, moving toward the door.

"What are you going to do?"

"I'm going to get rid of the sheriff, and then talk to Pete."

He moved quickly, catching her by the arm.

"Brenda, I don't think that's a good idea. Don't tell Pete anything about what we've discussed."

"Pete loves me, Canyon," she said. "He wouldn't hurt me."

"Would you have thought him capable of hurting your father?"

She thought a moment and then said, "No . . . and I still can't believe that he did." She looked at him and said, "I have to find out for myself, and the only way I can do that is to ask him."

"Brenda—"

"Just wait here," she said. "You'll be safe in the house."

She slipped from his grasp and went out the door. He wasn't so sure that he was safe in the house. He remembered a rifle mounted on the wall in the den, and left the office to get it.

"There's Brenda," Pete Gentry said.

Sheriff Festin and Gentry watched her as she approached them.

"Something I can do for you, Sheriff?" she asked.

"That fella you hired killed Red Atkins yesterday, Miss Edderly," Festin said. "I'm afraid he might come out here to hide. Have you seen him?"

"Not for a couple of days, I'm afraid," she said. "Are you sure he killed Red?"

"Positive."

"Maybe Red deserved it."

"He murdered him, Miss Edderly," Festin said, "pure and simple. It wouldn't be a good idea for you to try and help him."

"I'll decide that when the time comes, Sheriff," she said. "Right now I assure you I haven't see him. I have to talk to Pete. Would you excuse us?"

"I think I'll just have a look around before I leave," Festin said.

"Fine," she said.

Festin moved away from them, walking toward the livery stable.

"Brenda," Gentry said, "if you know where O'Grady is—"

"Pete," she said, cutting him off, "did you have anything to do with killing my father?"

"Brenda," Gentry said, patiently, "your father died by accident—"

"No, he didn't," she said. "He was murdered because he was going to sell the ranch—and you knew that, didn't you?" She stared at him, starting to realize that it had to be Gentry who had told the others about the sale. "You probably told the people in town—Burke, the town council—didn't you?"

"Brenda—"

"Tell me, Pete," she said. "Did you kill my father? Did you get him killed?"

"Brenda, I swear—" he began, and for a moment she thought he was going to confess, but then he stopped talking as something dawned on him. "O'Grady told you all of that, didn't he?"

"I haven't seen him—"

"He's in the house now, ain't he?"

"Pete—"

"Festin!" Gentry shouted. "Hey, Cal!"

Festin came out of the stable and Gentry started running toward him.

"He's in the house," he shouted. "He's in the god-damned house!"

Brenda ran toward the house.

"Stop her!" Festin shouted.

Gentry stopped short, turned, and saw Brenda, then started after her. If she had been a little closer to the house, or if Gentry's strides hadn't been so long, she might have made it, but he caught up to her just as she reached the front steps.

"Let me go!" she said, struggling.

"I can't let you go in there, Brenda," Gentry said, "you might get hurt."

"What do you care?" she demanded. "You killed my father. You all killed him!"

"I didn't, Brenda," Gentry said. "I swear it wasn't me who killed him."

"But you knew about it, didn't you? Didn't you?"

Festin reached them at that point and said, "Get someone to watch her, and then get the rest of the men over here. We've got to cover all the doors and windows so he can't get out, and then we'll go in after him."

"You stay out of my house, you murderer!" Brenda shouted. It wasn't clear who she was shouting at, Gentry or Festin, or both.

"Be quiet, Brenda," Festin said, "or you could end up like your father."

"You bastard!"

"Get her away from here, Pete," Festin said. "We've got work to do."

"I'll get the others," Gentry said. He looked at Brenda, who was glaring at him with naked hatred, and he said, "I'm sorry, Brenda."

She spat in his face.

O'Grady witnessed the whole thing from a front window, holding Harlan Edderly's rifle in his hands. He knew he had time to get out the back door, but after that he'd be in the open. He might be better off just staying in the house. When they came in after him they wouldn't come all at once. Festin would have to leave some men outside to cover the windows and doors.

Maybe, he thought, this will work for me rather than against me.

Maybe . . .

He had some time before they got organized, and he decided he'd use it to get to know the house.

Gentry handed Brenda over to one of his men, which left five other men for him to use. With him and Festin, that made seven.

"Let's put one man in the back, one in the front, and one on either side," Festin said to Gentry. "You, me, and the other man will go in after him."

"Hey," the man said, "I signed on to punch cows—"

"You signed on to do as you're told," Gentry said. "Understand?"

The man hesitated, then said, "Sure, boss."

"This man is wanted for murder," Festin said to all six of the men. "You men are duly deputized to help me bring him in."

Gentry dispatched the other men and then stood next to Festin.

"Is there anyone else likely to be in the house?" Festin asked.

"Maybe the cook," Gentry said.

"Watch out for her," Festin said. "If she gets killed we can always blame that on O'Grady, too, but let's try to avoid it."

"Right."

"All right," Festin said, "let's go in."

O'Grady quickly covered the first floor, noting where each room was, and how many entrances there were. In the kitchen he came upon the cook, a portly woman in her fifties who regarded him suspiciously while she dried her hands on her apron.

"Ma'am," he said, "I think it would be wise if you left the house."

"Where is Miss Edderly?" she demanded.

"Outside, Ma'am," he said, "which is where you should be."

"Why?"

"There's going to be some shooting."

"In the house?"

"I'm afraid so."

"Oh, my," she said.

"Go out the front door, Ma'am," he said. "They'll let you out."

"Oh, my," she said again.

"Is there anyone else in the house?" he asked.

"N-no," she said, "no one else."

"All right, then," he said, "you'd best be going."

She stared at him for a moment, then said, "Thank you," and went past him. At the door to the kitchen she stopped, looked at him and said, "Good luck."

"Thank you, Ma'am," he said. "I'm sure going to need it."

She started to leave, then stopped again.

"Mister?"

"Yes?"

"Are you the man tryin' to find out what happened to Mr. Edderly?"

"Yes, Ma'am, I am."

"Was he killed?"

"Yes, he was."

She thought about that for a moment, then said, "In that case, there's somethin' you should know about . . ."

23

To his credit, Cal Festin went through the front door first, followed by Pete Gentry and the third man, Rod Crowley. Just as Festin opened the door, however, the cook appeared in the doorway.

"Come on, Molly," Gentry said, "get out of there."

"Yes, sir."

"Where is he?" Festin stopped her and asked her.

"I don't know, Sheriff," she said. "He was in the kitchen."

"All right," he said, and allowed her to continue on until she was away from the house.

Inside, Festin said, "We'll split up. I'm going to take the kitchen. Pete, cover the other side of the house. You, check upstairs."

Crowley looked worried but, gun in hand, he went up the steps to the second floor.

"Pete," Festin said.

"Yeah?"

"Where's the kitchen?" Festin had never been in the house before.

"Through the dining room, right through there," Gentry said.

"All right," Festin said. "Let's do this."

They searched the house and met up again in the main hallway.

"Anything?" Festin asked Crowley as he came down the steps.

"No."

"Did you check under the beds?" the sheriff asked.

Crowley nodded and said, "And in the closets."

"Pete?"

"Nothing, Cal," Gentry said.

"Stay here," Festin said to them. "I'll check with the men outside."

Festin went out and returned in a few minutes.

"Well?" Gentry said.

"They haven't seen him," Festin said. "He couldn't have gotten away from the house that fast."

"Then where is he?" Gentry asked.

"I don't know," Festin said. "We're gonna look again. I'll take the upstairs this time, Pete, you take the kitchen. You check the other side of the house," he said to Crowley, whose name he hadn't bothered to ask.

"Yes, sir."

They went through the house again. Festin felt silly looking under the beds and in the closets. He checked the ceilings to see if there was any access to the roof, but there were no trap doors or hatches that O'Grady could have gone through.

In the kitchen, Gentry looked in pantries and closets, and even stuck his head out the back door.

Crowley checked the den and office with no luck. He paused to snitch a small sip of brandy from a crystal decanter in the office, then went back to the main hallway.

"Nothing," Festin said. "That isn't possible. Pete, go outside and tell the others to check the ground. Have two of them mount up and ride away from the house. If he did get away from the house, he's either on foot, or he's riding Mary Chaplin's old buggy horse. Either way, he can't be that far from the house."

"Right."

"We'll wait here," Festin said to Crowley.

"Crowley," the man said.

"What?"

"My name's Crowley."

"Whatever," Festin said.

When Pete Gentry came back in he said, "What do we do now?"

"We go through the house again," Festin said. "Take upstairs, Pete, and I'll take this side. You—"

"Crowley," Crowley said.

"Yeah, whatever," Festin said, "check the dining room and the kitchen."

They split up again, checked their own portions of the house, and returned to the hallway. At least Festin and Gentry returned.

"Where's the other man?" Festin asked.

"Crowley?"

"Yes, Crowley," Festin said, annoyed. "Who else would I be asking about? Where is he?"

"I don't know," Gentry said. "He went to check the kitchen."

"Come on," Festin said, and led the way through the dining room into the kitchen. There was nobody there.

"Shit," Festin said. He went to the back door and looked out, then came back inside.

"Now he's gone," Festin said. "What the hell—wait a minute."

"What?" Gentry asked.

"You know this house," Festin said. "Has it got a root cellar?"

Gentry thought a minute, then said, "I don't know."

"Look around," Festin said. "There's got to be something."

They started inspecting the floor closely, running their hands over the floorboards until Festin finally found something.

"Wait," he said, "here."

Gentry turned and watched as Festin put his gun away, dug his fingers in and pried open a door in the

165

floor. Festin opened it, then backed away and took out his gun again.

"Come on out, O'Grady," he called down. "We know you're down there."

There was no reply.

"O'Grady!"

Nothing.

"Maybe he ain't down there," Gentry said.

"Is there a lamp around here?"

"Over here," Gentry said, unhooking a storm lamp from the wall.

"Light the damn thing."

Gentry lit the lamp and asked, "Who's going down?"

"Give me the damn thing!" Festin said. "I'll go down. Cover me."

He took the lamp from Gentry and held it in his left hand.

"I'm coming down, O'Grady," he called out. "If you kill me, Gentry will kill you."

By the light of the lamp he could see that there was a wooden ladder leading down to the cellar. He tried to go down frontward but couldn't. He finally had to turn his back to go down.

Gentry moved to the opening and looked down. He saw Festin reach the bottom and then turn around.

"Is he there?" Gentry asked.

"Goddamnit!" Festin swore.

"What is it?" Gentry asked. "Is he there?"

"He ain't here," Festin called up, "but Crowley is."

"Is he dead?"

"He should be," Festin said, "but he ain't. I'm coming up."

At that point a closet—one that had been searched twice already—opened and O'Grady stepped out, pointing his gun at Gentry.

"Tell him not to bother," he said.

*   *   *

166

Outside the house, Molly the cook and Brenda Edderly stood in the stable with a man watching both of them.

"You'll be fired after this, you know," Brenda told him.

"I'm just followin' orders, Ma'am."

"I pay you," she said. "Whose orders do you think you should be following?"

"I'm a ranch hand, Ma'am," the man said, almost apologetically. "I follow my foreman's orders."

"What's going on, Ma'am?" Molly asked.

"The foreman of this ranch," Brenda said, "and the sheriff of the town, along with who knows who else, conspired to kill my father and make it look like an accident."

"But . . . why?" she asked.

"So he wouldn't sell the ranch."

"What?" the man asked.

"What's your name?" Brenda asked him.

"Tim, Ma'am," he said, "Tim Mathis."

"Well, Tim," she said, "if you let me leave this stable now, you may not only keep your job, but stay out of jail."

"But . . . I thought Mr. Edderly died by accident?" Mathis said.

"That's what it was supposed to look like," she said. "Oh, Jesus, what's going on in that house? I'm going out to take a look."

"Ma'am—"

"You'll have to shoot me to stop me, Tim," she said, and walked out of the stable.

"Me, too," Molly said haughtily, and followed Brenda out.

Tim Mathis didn't know what to do, so he followed them out.

In front of the house, Brenda saw the other four men. They had their guns out and were obviously waiting for orders.

She heard horses approaching, turned, and saw about half a dozen riders coming toward them. More men from town.

"Great," she said, "now Canyon is dead."

And for all she knew, so was she.

"What the hell—" Gentry said.

"Just tell him to stay down there," O'Grady said, "and get rid of your gun."

"Better stay down there, Sheriff," Gentry called out.

"What for?"

"Because O'Grady is up here and he's got a gun on me," Gentry said.

"Your gun," O'Grady said. "Toss it."

Gentry tossed his gun aside, away from him.

"O'Grady," Festin called from down below, "you're a dead man."

"Maybe," O'Grady said, "but you won't live to see me die unless you toss your gun up here."

"No chance."

"You have to come up sometime, Sheriff."

"By that time the other men will be back," Festin said. "You've got no chance, O'Grady."

O'Grady moved closer to Gentry and pressed the barrel of Harlan Edderly's rifle against the back of the foreman's head.

"If he doesn't come up," he said, "you're dead."

"Jesus," Gentry said, "come on up, Cal!"

"He won't kill you, Pete."

"Cal!"

"It's a stand-off, O'Grady," Festin called. O'Grady saw the light go out. The sheriff had probably blown it out to gain the protection of the dark. "Tell me something. How did you know about this root cellar?"

"The cook told me before she went out," O'Grady said. "Seems she, Brenda, and old Harlan were the only ones who knew about it."

"And you were down here the whole time?"

"That's right, until you sent that other man into the kitchen. Then I switched places with him. He should be waking up anytime now, Sheriff, but don't expect any help from him. I've got his gun up here."

"You're still a dead man, O'Grady," Festin's disembodied voice said.

"How long can you stay down there, Sheriff?"

"As long as it takes for the rest of the men to decide to come into the house to see what's going on."

O'Grady knew he was right. The other men would become impatient and come inside soon enough. He also knew that he wasn't going to shoot Pete Gentry in cold blood.

"Tell me something, Festin," O'Grady said, "whose idea was it to kill Edderly?"

"I don't know," Festin said, "somebody came up with it, and the rest of us just went along with it. It seemed like a good idea at the time."

"Who actually killed him?"

"Ha!" Festin said. "Somebody who was able to get real close to him."

O'Grady prodded Pete Gentry with the rifle and said, "You? His foreman? He gave you a job, Gentry."

"And if he sold the ranch, I'd lose it," Gentry said. "What was I supposed to do? But it was Festin who came to me with the idea."

"The council came up with it," Festin said. "My part was approaching Gentry with it."

"What a waste of a man's life," O'Grady said. "The ranch probably would have gone on just as before, whoever bought it. Now Brenda probably will sell it."

"She won't do that," Gentry said, although he didn't sound very sure of himself. "I can make her see."

"Not after she finds out you killed her father,"

O'Grady said, prodding him with the rifle. "All she'll want then is to see you hang."

"Festin," Gentry called out, "do something."

"I am," Festin said, chuckling. "I'm waiting."

"Jesus—" Gentry said.

Suddenly, they all heard the front door open, and it was obvious from the footsteps that more than one person had entered the house.

"Here they come, O'Grady," Festin called. "You better go out the back door and run."

O'Grady was considering that when he heard Brenda's voice.

"Canyon? Where are you?"

"In the kitchen," he called back.

"What's going on?" Festin demanded. "What's she doing in here?"

Brenda came into the kitchen followed by Mary Chaplin and Steve Stilwell. Nick McLish was also there.

"What's happening?" Festin called out.

"I don't know," O'Grady said. He looked at Stilwell and said, "What is happening?"

"It's over," Stilwell said. "Mary came to me and told me the whole story, and I ran this off."

He held up a copy of the newspaper he published, *The Little Bend Gazette*. The front page said HARLAN EDDERLY MURDERED.

O'Grady looked at McLish, who shrugged.

"I go on to name names," Stilwell said. "Festin, Gentry, Burke, McLish, the entire town council. I've already sent a batch of papers out of town, so they can't be stopped. By tomorrow, the story will be all over the place. There won't be any point to anyone else being killed." He gave O'Grady a concerned look and said, "I'm hoping that it's true, that we can prove it."

"We can," O'Grady said, smiling. He looked down into the dark hole in the floor and called out, "Festin?

You better light that lamp again. You've got some reading to do."

O'Grady stayed in Little Bend until the help he had sent for arrived in the person of a federal marshal named Page. He left his warm hotel bed—with Candy still in it—when the deputy knocked on his door and announced that the marshal had arrived. When he got to the sheriff's office, Page was sitting behind the desk. Stilwell was present, as was Brenda Edderly, and the deputy.

"These people have been telling me an interesting story, Mr. O'Grady," Page said. He also had Stilwell's newspaper in front of him, and he was fingering it.

"It's all true, Marshal."

"Yes, I'm sure it is," he said. He was a tall, dark-haired man with broad shoulders and a long jaw. "I understand the entire town council is locked up in these cells."

"They are," O'Grady said. "The deputy here had nothing to do with the killing, so we had him lock up all of the guilty parties."

In the cells were McLish, King, Decker, Jarrod Burke, Pete Gentry, and several other members of the town council of Little Bend who had voted to kill Harlan Edderly rather than allow him to sell his ranch.

"One of them actually killed Harlan Edderly, but the others were all involved in the conspiracy to kill him," O'Grady said. "In fact, some of them will testify to that fact in the hopes of some sort of reduced punishment."

"Good luck to them. In fact, this entire town would seem to need a helluva lot of luck to survive," Page observed. "Miss Edderly, I understand you're selling your ranch?"

"That's right, Marshal," she said, looking at O'Grady. "All I want to do is get away from here. I don't care if the town dies."

"It may very well do that," the marshal said. He gave O'Grady a look that said, "We'll talk later." They didn't know each other, but the marshal knew that O'Grady worked for the government. He was smart enough not to let on in front of the others.

"And what about the sheriff?" Page asked. "If there's anything I can't stand, it's a lawman gone bad. Why isn't he in a cell?"

"Well," O'Grady said, exchanging a glance with Brenda, "he is locked up, sort of. You'll just have to go out to the ranch to get him."

Festin still had not come up out of the root cellar, and as far as O'Grady and Brenda were concerned, he could take root there.